LEGACY OF THE NECROMANCER

LEGACY OF THE NECROMANCER

J. D. ROBINSON

TYPESET PRESS

Copyright © 2020 by J. D. Robinson

All rights reserved.

No part of this book may be reproduced in any form or by any electronic or mechanical means, including information storage and retrieval systems, without written permission from the author, except for the use of brief quotations in a book review.

*To all my readers.
You mean the world to me.*

Chapter 1

I let out a breath of relief and set my pen down. That wasn't nearly as bad as I had feared it would be. Glancing around the auditorium at the other students taking the same Calculus exam, there were empty seats scattered around. John had already left. A few finished papers sat on Professor Redding's table down in the front of the room. At least I wasn't the first one finished. That was usually a bad sign for my grades.

I checked to make sure my name was on my exam and stood to gather my things before heading down the stairs to turn in my final.

"Have a good holiday, Mr. Stanwood," Professor Redding said as I added my papers to the stack. He looked up at me over the nearly destroyed copy of a romance novel. It was the same one he'd read during all of our exams this semester.

"You too, Professor. See you next year."

He arched an eyebrow up at me and returned to his book as I left.

My roommate was waiting for me out in the hallway. A tall and lanky kid, John was always hungry. I'd never see anyone eat as much as he did and stay skinny.

"Hey man, how'd you do?" he said, standing from the spot he'd claimed on a nearby bench.

"Okay, I guess? I don't feel horrible about it."

"Let's head back, you probably want to drop that bag of books off before we do anything else."

Readjusting the strap of my bag, I moved it higher up on my shoulder. I thought it'd be a good idea to get some last-minute studying in before the exam, but I was too nervous to concentrate.

John trudged alongside me as we discussed the horrible selection of questions Professor Redding had chosen. The dorms and the cafeteria were on the other side of the campus, but it really wasn't a bad walk. The sun had set while we were in the exam, turning the snow-covered campus into a dark and silent place. I always loved this time of night, when the university was still, and the cold silence reminded me of the dark forests that surrounded my home. It made me homesick even though there was nowhere else I'd rather be other than here.

"So, you in for game night tonight?" John asked, pulling me from my thoughts.

I shrugged. "You know I'm not really great at those drinking games you play."

He slapped my shoulder with his hand, shaking my entire frame. "That's why we invite you, Ez! Besides, we've got to work on that tolerance of yours. You would think being from the country and all, you'd have better drinking habits than all of us, especially with those parents of yours."

Laughing with him, I kept my excuses to myself. It was easier to blame strict parents than to try and explain the truth: that alcohol could lead to some deadly consequences in my family's line of work. Dad had warned my brother and me against drinking since we were little, explaining some of the disasters he'd seen in his youth.

"I should probably clean up and study for my last exam," I said instead.

"Whatever," John said as we turned the last corner to our building. "It's not like you don't have all week to do that."

A loud shriek of a bird called out over the little square between the buildings. The familiar sound froze me in my tracks and automatically sent my gaze searching the trees for its source.

"You coming?" John yelled. He stood with the door to our dorm open, waiting for me to climb the steps.

"Uh, no." I shook my head. "I just remembered I need to go back, uh, to the library. I need to find a book. For my history exam." Gods above and below, that sounded lame, even for me.

John gave a look that he'd given me a lot this past semester. One that went with him shaking his head and muttering something about crazy country folk. Again, it was easier to let him make his own assumptions about my oddities than to explain the truth.

"Right, see you later, then." He shut the door behind him, the automated lock clicking into place.

I waited a moment more, making sure that he wouldn't turn back, before walking around the edge of the building to the little wooded area that separated the dorms from the parking lots. The bird called again, a different sound this time, one that I was even more familiar with. I lifted my arm as a large black shape swooped down from one of the pine trees, landing on my arm with a gentle squeeze of his claws. I hugged the raven to my chest, tears pricking at my eyes.

"Poe, what in the world are you doing here?" I whispered.

He rubbed his head under my chin, his beak nipping at the hair pushed behind my ear.

"I missed you, too, but that doesn't explain why you're here."

The raven straightened, shaking out its feathers in a gesture that could only be described as a shrug.

"Poe," I said, finding it hard to be stern when I was so relieved and happy to see him. It'd been weeks since my last trip home.

Poe tilted his head, then bent to peck at one of his metal bracelets. The longer one on his right leg was meant to hold messages. I released the clasp on it and pulled out the tiny scroll of paper that was wrapped inside. Poe jumped up to my shoulder, his favorite perch, as I pulled out my outdated cell phone to read the scroll by its light.

Ezra, your presence is required at home. Please return immediately.

The note was signed by William Stanwood, the Head of the Stanwood Family. My father. It was a direct order I couldn't refuse. My shoulders felt tight as I allowed the paper to roll-up before shoving it in my jacket pocket. Something must have happened at home.

Staring at the lights of my university and the city beyond it, I fought the emerging pain in my chest. This past semester I'd been normal. I'd fit in. Well, kinda fit in. There was only so much I could do to fit into modern society when I'd grown-up without most common conveniences like computers or cell phones. We didn't have any reception for those on our mountain. But here, I'd started to find myself. I only hoped I'd be allowed to return.

I left Poe in the square and returned to my room to gather what I needed to take home. I packed the few personal items I'd brought with me. Clothes were a given, considering I'd brought the only few sets I owned. I also grabbed my textbooks and notes for the exam on Friday, in the hope that I might make it back in time to actually take my exam.

John had already left, so I scribbled a quick post-it note on his microwave - a place I know he'd see it soon and went down to the student parking lot.

Poe was already waiting for me on the luggage rack of my beat-up SUV. It had horrible gas mileage, but it got me around. I tossed my bag in the back seat and pulled the tattered plaid blanket from the trunk for Poe, curling it into a makeshift nest in the passenger seat before lowering him into the car. It wasn't the first time we'd road-tripped like this, and I'm sure it wouldn't be the last. I climbed in and started the car. Taking a deep breath, I checked to make sure I had everything I needed.

"Time to go home."

The orange glow of dawn peeked over the trees as I pulled my car up the long driveway. I'd driven through the night, only stopping briefly in the town closest to my family's house, to get gas and a bite to eat, but that was an hour ago. I was so ready to crawl into bed.

I forced my eyes wide as I turned the last corner of the drive, and the house finally came into view. Nestled among the trees, my parent's house was perched precariously on the side of the mountain that overlooked the valley and river below. No matter how often I thought that I didn't belong here, it still called to me. This was home. It always would be.

There were two cars with out-of-state tags parked in front of the house. I didn't recognize them, but I had a sinking feeling that something was wrong. We never had visitors, especially ones from out of town.

I parked and gathered Poe into my arms before climbing out of the car. The kitchen door on the side of the house opened before I'd taken even two steps towards it.

"I thought I heard you," Mom's voice called as she stepped

out onto the little step. She was wearing her favorite yellow dress, the one with the tiny white polka dots that Dad had surprised her with for her birthday a few years back. It'd always reminded me of pictures of those perfect 1950's housewives, but I'd never dare tell her that. Dad may have been the Head of the Stanwood Family, but there was no doubt who ruled the house.

"I got Dad's message," I said, releasing Poe, letting him fly up to the trees that he'd roosted in as long as I had been around. I turned to Mom, giving in to the hug I knew she'd want. Her arms wrapped around me, pulling me in tight.

"I'm glad you're home," she whispered, with a sadness to her voice that wasn't normal.

"What's going on?" I asked. "Who's here?"

She released me and pulled me into the kitchen. My eyes fell on the girl who sat at the table. She was about my age, her strawberry blonde hair twisted back away from her face in messy braids, and her hands wrapped tightly around a mug of coffee. She looked up at me as I stepped in, and as soon as those tear-filled crystal blue eyes rested on me, I knew exactly who she was.

"Avery."

I hadn't seen her since we were what, seven years old? We had stayed in touch, writing letters to each other. But that intimacy of knowing her without actually seeing her had not prepared me for this.

She stood, rushing over to fling herself at me as she sobbed into my shoulder. "What's wrong?"

Holding her awkwardly in my arms, I looked to my mother with the hope she'd tell me what the hell was going on.

Mom wrung her hands on her apron, tears threatening to spill over her own cheeks. "Mr. Manser has passed on."

I tightened my grip on Avery as she cried harder at my

mother's words. Caleb Manser, her father. The Head of the Manser family. And now that he was gone...

Raised voices spilled out from Dad's study down the hall, but I couldn't quite make out what the argument was about. I had a good idea, though. The Manser family was like my own, part of the Necromantic Circle. With the Caleb Manser gone, it was time to choose the new Head of the Manser family. And that brought on a whole new set of problems.

Avery stepped back, wiping her eyes. "I'm sorry, Ezra. It's only been a few days, but I just keep hoping I'll wake up."

I pulled her back to me, hugging her tightly. "It's okay," I whispered, not even trying to imagine what she was going through. The thought of losing my dad was too much for me to even hypothesize.

The sound of gravel crunching out on the driveway drew my mother to peer out the window over the sink. "It's Nathan. Finally, we were expecting him hours ago."

My stomach rolled. From worse news to atomic. Nathan Ackland despised me, and I thanked the gods every time the families met that my name wasn't listed in the Ackland's family tree.

Mom turned back to us, undoing the straps on her apron as she spoke. "Erza, why don't you show Avery where the bathroom is, so she can freshen up. We'll be getting started soon." Mom gave me a look that I knew all too well. It was time to make ourselves scarce, and I didn't mind. The less time I spent in Nathan's line of sight, the better.

"Sure," I said and steered Avery down the hall past Dad's study. It was probably my most cherished place in the entire house. I had spent hours in there every day as I was growing up, reading all of the Stanwood books, and studying my family's history. There had been nearly as many nights that I'd spent listening to my father and brother discuss necromantic theories with me offering input as I could.

From the sound of the voices inside, Avery's mother, Evelyn, and Lyssa, the Head of the Amerson family, were arguing about marriages. Avery hurried past, her hand tightly interlaced with mine as she pulled me along. We ran up the stairs as the sound of the kitchen's screen door slammed shut.

Tip-toeing down the hall, we went up another flight of stairs to the finished attic that was my room. I shut the door behind us and turned to see Avery taking a seat on my bed. It dawned on me that this was the first time I'd ever had a girl in my room.

I looked around, trying to find anything to keep my hands busy, and settled for tidying my desk. It was the only part of my room I hadn't picked up before I'd left the last time I visited.

"Ezra?" Avery's voice was soft.

I glanced back to see her motioning for me to join her. I set the papers down, and shuffled over to the bed, awkwardly wrapping my arm around her shoulders. She leaned into me.

"It's still there," she whispered, resting her head against my chest.

My body froze of its own accord as she looked up, her face kissably close.

"You are a necromancer," she said, "even if your power refuses to manifest."

I stared at her, at the clarity in her eyes. The Manser family was known for their prophecies and seeing things that only they could understand. And she was the only one in all the families to believe that I had any sort of power.

"And here I thought you were just being nice to the poor, Talentless kid." I grinned at her, trying not to show the pain talking about my powers, or lack thereof caused. She had more than enough to worry about at the moment.

Avery pulled back with a quiet, knowing expression on her face. She took my hand into her own and studied it, tracing the lines along my palm. I waited, content to just be beside her now that the shock of her sudden appearance had worn off. I'd missed her, and I hadn't even realized how much until now.

"I missed you," I whispered the words to her, afraid of what she might say in return.

She looked up at me, the smallest of smiles touching her lips. "I missed you, too."

A comfortable silence settled over us, one that I thought wouldn't have been possible, as she continued to trace the patterns of my palm.

"Do you remember the last time you were here? For the Family summit?" I asked her, pulling my hand from her gentle fingers and standing. I walked over and opened my closet, reaching for a box on the top shelf.

"Yeah, how could I forget it?" she said with a small laugh. "All the kids were forced to put on that horrible play. The one about the Families coming together and the war with the Witches."

I set the box on the floor of the closet to open it, keeping my back to her so she couldn't see that it was filled with her letters.

"And Collen Ackland threw up in the middle of it." I finally pulled the photo free from under the letters and replaced the lid on the box. I turned and reclaimed my seat next to her on the bed.

"Oh jeez, Ezra! I can't believe you still have that!" She blushed and nudged me with her shoulder.

"It's the only photo of you I have."

She took the picture from me, looking it over. It showed a seven-year-old Avery, dressed up as Mary Annabelle Manser, one of the founders of the Necromantic Circle. She was standing impishly in front of the barn door, next to the other kids. I was hidden in the back of the group behind my older brother. As the youngest, and the fact that I still hadn't shown a hint of power, I was given the only role in the play that didn't require the use of Talent.

"I still can't believe they dressed you up as a tree," she said.

We laughed together, and it was beautiful to see a smile on her face, even if it was brief. Avery and I had been inseparable when she visited. It felt as though she was supposed to be by my side, standing with me against anything the world could throw at us. But the reality of her situation was sinking in.

"Who do you think they'll choose?" I asked her quietly. If they chose her to take her father's place-

I really didn't want to think about what would happen next. Because it certainly couldn't involve me.

She shrugged and drew her knees up to hug them. She started to say something, but then stopped herself, looking away from me.

I adjusted my position on the bed, turning more to look at her. "You've seen something, haven't you?"

"No, I didn't." She lowered her gaze, suddenly more interested in the geometric patterns on my bedspread. "Someone else did."

"What was it?"

She hesitated, and in that breath of a moment, there was a knock at the door.

"Avery?" a little voice called.

"You can come in, Thea," Avery said, and we watched the door open to show a copy of the girl in the photo, even down to the exact color of her eyes. Eyes that widened a fraction when they landed on me.

She stood in the doorway as if she was afraid of coming closer. "Avery, mommy asked me to come get you and Ezra. They want to start the meeting."

Avery stood. "Okay, thank you."

I watched Thea race off down the hall to the stairs, unnerved by the presence of the little girl. There was something about her that struck me as odd. "I remember you talking about your sister in your letters, but she-"

"She's the most powerful of all the Mansers," Avery said, turning back to me. "Even Dad's power couldn't match hers. It's scary seeing her with all that. She will be Head of the Family someday, but Mom doesn't want to force it on her too soon. I think she's hoping to handle things until Thea is old enough to take on that responsibility." She left it unsaid, but the worry was plain on her face. If they didn't let Evelyn ascend to leadership, it would fall to Avery.

"I thought I'd have more time. I'm not ready," she whispered, "I'm not ready to bond with someone I don't know."

I couldn't think of anything that to say that could possibly make her feel any better.

"Come on, we don't want to keep them waiting." I pulled her toward the door, and we followed Thea downstairs.

My father's study was too small to hold all of the adults and the 'kids,' so they'd moved to the living room. Avery released my hand before turning the corner as if she were afraid of their judgment. I couldn't blame her. The Families tended to look down on interfering with each other's affairs, and unmarried relations even more so. Arranged marriages were a completely different story, though, since they were a way to ensure that children continued to be born with necromantic talent. We kept meticulous genealogy records and brought in enough fresh blood to keep our Family lines strong.

Avery left my side to go stand by her mother and sister, who sat on the far couch with my mother. My father stood near the fireplace mantle with my older brother, Liam, and Lyssa, the Head of the Amerson family, only a short step behind him.

"Ezra," Nathan said, his voice flat and cold. He stood on

the opposite side of the fire from my father in one of his expensive business suits. His son Collen stood behind him like a shadow. "I thought you went away... to school. How pleasant that you can join us. What was it you decided to study again?"

"Chemistry," I said, taking a seat on the piano bench in the back of the room.

Nathan gave me a look of contempt. "There's no point to have you here. A Talentless shouldn't be privileged to the information we'll be discussing here."

"My father summoned me, and so I came." As a Talentless, I would have no say in what would be decided here today. But if the Head of my Family wanted me here for such an important family decision, I would be. What else could I do?

He turned to my father and pointed a finger at me. "He needs to leave."

This was why I had hated Nathan Ackland since I was old enough to understand what the word meant. Well, to be honest, maybe I didn't hate him. I just disliked him very, *very* much.

My father's gaze turned icy, the frown lines deepening around his eyes. "He may be Talentless, but he is still a member of the Stanwood Family, and I require him to be here."

And cue tension. The room was silent as the two most powerful Necromancers in the world stared each other down. I held my breath, waiting for Nathan to push the issue further. It was Avery's mother who broke the silence though, reaching out a willowy hand to touch Nathan's arm.

"Please, Nathan, just let it go. Don't we have enough to deal with today?" Evelyn barely whispered the words, but everyone heard them anyway.

"Fine," he said, but the glare he shot at me said that it was far from the end of the discussion I'd hear this visit. Lucky me.

Dad stepped forward, clearing his throat. "Let us begin this meeting by taking a moment to remember the life of our comrade, Caleb Manser."

The morning light filtered in through the curtains, tinting the room in the tawny grey of the cloth. As everyone else bowed their heads in respect, I surveyed the gathering. In this little living room, on a shabby mountaintop cabin, were the precious few people in the country who had mastered the necromantic arts. My father and brother were the last two living with enough power to reanimate the dead. Avery and Thea Manser had Sight, the ability to see truths and that of the present and future. Lyssa Amerson carried her family's ability to speak with the dead and the spirits from beyond. And then there was Nathan. His family possessed the skills and knowledge of Blood Rituals and other blood magics.

Even my mother and Avery's mother, Evelyn, had power. Although theirs was nowhere near as powerful as the others. Everyone here was a necromancer. Everyone, except me.

"He was a friend, a husband, a father," Dad continued. "And a necromancer of priceless ability. Caleb Manser, the sixty-third Head of the Manser Family, will forever be looked upon as an Elder of our Circle, and a great man. May the Great Ones take care of his soul."

Mrs. Manser's quiet sobs filled the space of silence after my father's words. Avery glanced up at me through tear-filled eyes, her hand tightly gripping one of her mother's. I'd do anything to take her pain from her. Even if I had the Talent to bring her father back, he wouldn't be the same. His soul would have moved on when he passed, so if he was brought back, it would only be his physical body and not the loving father she remembered.

Nathan stepped forward, standing next to my father, and the differences between them couldn't have been more evident than night and day. Where my father was tall and muscular from hard mountain work, Nathan Ackland was smaller than average height and thin enough to look like he was always sick. And the hardest he'd ever worked at anything was blocking me from any of the Circle's gatherings.

"It's time to place the past behind us and move forward with choosing our future." Nathan turned to Avery and her mother. "Evelynn, you stepped forward, and it has been discussed and agreed upon that you cannot claim the title of the Manser Family. Even though you possess talent, you are a Manser in name only."

I felt the tension in Avery rise from clear across the room. Nathan was right though, I'd read through all of the Laws set down by the Families. It was very clearly stated that the Heads of the Family must carry the family's blood.

"But that's not fair!" she shouted. "My mother has given everything for our family."

"It's alright, Avery," Evelyn said in a soothing, but still raw voice.

"No, Mom, it's not!" Avery pulled her hand away to stand and stared Nathan down.

He kept his calm, and they stared each other in the eye. "Avery Manser," he continued. "It has been discussed and agreed upon that you are the next in line worthy and of age to accept the title 'Head of the Manser Family.'"

I watched the color drain from Avery's face. I stood, ready to go and comfort her as Nathan added a stipulation.

"We can offer you this only on one condition."

"And what would that be?" Avery's voice was soft, afraid.

"On the conclusion of your bonding ceremony." Nathan grinned with pleasure. I knew that this was his idea, and the only reason he was so happy about it was because he was going to get something he wanted out of the deal.

I started forward, but movement from the corner of my vision caught my attention. Liam, my brother, had taken a step in my direction. When he saw that he had my attention, he shook his head, warning me not to interfere.

"Yes, as the next Head of the Family, you must marry and continue the line. If you can not," he glanced at Thea, "then the line will pass to your sister when she turns eighteen and is married. Until that time, the Manser Family would be under the protection and guidance of the Circle, as our laws state."

Thea's gaze was focused on her hands in her lap.

"And who should I marry?" Avery demanded. "Have you figured all that out, too?" She glanced around at my father and Lyssa.

"We do have a suggestion as to whom may be a good candidate for an arrangement," Lyssa finally said, slowly.

"And who, pray tell, might I have the privilege of being engaged to?" Avery said each word carefully, anger controlling the features of her face as I fought for breath.

Nathan smiled, and it wasn't a happy one. More like a devil looking at the soul of his latest binding contract. "My youngest son, Collen, would be an excellent match. Our two lines haven't been joined in nearly three generations. It would be a union of unmatched possibilities-"

"NO!"

Everyone turned to Thea, who glared up at us from her seat on the couch. "No, that's not how it's supposed to be!" She jumped up and rushed over to me, pulling me by the hand until I stood next to Avery. "They're supposed to be together."

Nathan rolled his eyes, stepping away. "This is unbelievable."

Evelyn reached out, pulling her youngest daughter closer to her. "Thea, this isn't the time to be playing."

"I'm not playing, Mommy. I saw it." She turned her eyes to us, daring anyone to challenge her. "I saw it."

I glanced at Avery, but her attention was firmly fixed on her little sister. I turned to my father then, unsure of what to do or say. This was happening faster than I could follow. I didn't want Avery to be forced into any marriage she wasn't comfortable with, even if it was with me.

My father stepped over, kneeling to be at her eye level. "Thea, I need you to tell us exactly what you saw," he said very carefully.

"Oh, you can not be seriously entertaining the fantasies of a child, William!" Nathan shouted.

"This child," father said, turning his gaze up to Nathan, "happens to be the most powerful psychic in the world at the moment. I think it would be wise to at least hear her words."

Nathan turned to Lyssa, but she merely shook her head at him. "I agree with William in this. We should listen to the girl, and consider our options very carefully."

He tsked, and stepped away, retreating to the fireplace and away from the rest of us as he sulked.

"Now, Thea," William started again, "start from the beginning. What did you see?"

"Them," she stated simply. "I saw Avery and Ezra. They," she paused and glanced around to her mother. "They were together, in bed."

I felt my face go six different shades of scarlet. I wanted to run and hide, but my feet felt glued to the floor.

"That doesn't prove anything," Nathan said, spinning around.

"That wasn't all," Thea continued. "It was like a picture flip book, like the one I got at the fair. They were getting married, then they were holding a baby. Then, they were planting, outside in a garden when something attacked them." She looked up at me. "You fought next to Avery, I can still see it. You used Talent to defend your future family."

I stared at her, unable to comprehend what she was telling me. She'd seen me use Talent? It wasn't possible, was it?

"There!" Nathan interjected. "That's proof that she's lying.

He doesn't have Talent! If it hasn't manifested by now, it never will."

"He does too have power!" Thea yelled. "It's different, and you're just too dumb to understand."

"Thea Rose Manser!" Evelyn reached for her, but Thea nimbly dodged and hid behind Avery.

I would have thought that hearing someone else say that I had power would have made me feel better, or less alone, but it made me feel worse. If I did have Talent, if I was a true necromancer like the rest of them, why hadn't it manifested yet?

"Why you little brat-" Nathan tried to reach for her as well, but Avery stood her ground between them.

"If you so much as touch her," she threatened.

"Hold on now," Dad chimed in, standing to try and persuade Nathan to back down.

Everyone was speaking at once, trying to be heard over one another. Thea screamed, and the room fell silent once again.

"If you don't believe me, test him," she said after a moment.

Everyone turned to look at me, and all I could do was stare back. There was no way I could pass the test, not without Talent.

I glanced down at Thea. "I know you mean well, but I don't think me taking the test is such a great idea."

"Oh, by all means, I think that is actually a most excellent idea," Nathan cooed. "That would solve quite a few problems, it would seem."

Yeah, I'm sure my death would solve several problems for Nathan. I gulped. The very last thing on this earth I wanted was to take that test. The test that I'd seen my brother take when he turned 18. The test that marked him as a full-fledged Necromancer of the Circle, and nearly killed him in the process. He wore the burn scars from it on his face and down the left side of his body.

"No," my mother cried. "William, don't make them do this. Don't let them kill our son!" Mom's plea to my father bothered me more than the actual threat of taking the test. Even she didn't think that I could do it.

"If he can pass the test, then I will retract my proposition of marriage between the Acklands and the Mansers. So that Ezra and Avery may be free to wed as the little prophet has foreseen, but if Ezra fails," Nathan said, and then paused. "Then, there is no other choice then, is there?"

I looked at Avery, catching her eyes with my own. Everything slowed down in that sappy, chick-flick kinda way, and I knew what I'd known since the first time I saw her. That I'd do anything for her, even if it meant certain death, I had to try.

Mom stepped in front of me as she went off at Nathan. Everyone was yelling and arguing, debating my fate without any input from me whatsoever. I glanced down at Thea, the only other person in the room who was quiet besides myself.

Thea met my gaze and nodded. She believed I could do it. She'd seen that I had.

"I'll do it," I said, and no one heard me over the noise. "HEY!"

They all turned to me, shock written on more than one face, the room silent. The old radiator kicked on, the loud grating noise echoing around us.

"I'll do it," I repeated. "I accept the challenge of the test."

Chapter 2

I reached into the backseat of my car and pulled my bag from the floorboard. The early morning sun had been hidden by dark, snow-heavy clouds, and the air was growing colder by the minute.

"You can't do this, Ezra. It's suicide!" Avery's voice was near hysterical.

I shut the door and turned to face her. I didn't know what to say. How could I tell her everything that I'd kept so buried in myself that I'd only just realized what it meant? How could I tell her that I was doing this for her because I loved her?

I dropped the bag at my feet, and I took her hands into my own. They trembled a little as I watched her take a deep breath.

"Ezra, I just lost my father, I..." she hesitated, gripping my hands hard. "I can't lose you, too."

She started crying again. I hugged her tight, wrapping my arms around her like I had earlier this morning. It was funny. I'd spent years sending letters to her, thinking of one day holding her like this, and now, I feared that this might actually be the last chance.

I took a slow breath as I watched the first flakes of snowfall around us. "I have to do this. I can't let Nathan jerk us around like puppets. He acts like the Circle is his to control."

She pulled away from me. "That has nothing to do with this."

"It has everything to do with it." I stepped back from her. "I won't stand by and watch you be forced to bond with and marry someone you don't love. If I can pass the test, then you'll be free to be with whoever you want. It wouldn't have to be me."

Avery stalked away from me, only to turn back with her hands clutched at her sides.

"But you don't have any power," she screamed. "How do you expect to complete the test without any Talent? You're going to die if you go through with this!"

I stared at her, as it dawned on her what she'd said. I bent down and picked up my bag. "I've got to get ready."

"Wait, Ezra," she said, "I didn't mean it like that."

I turned back to the house, as Poe glided down from the gutter to sit on my shoulder. I wouldn't look back, I couldn't. I didn't want her to see the tears in my eyes.

I went back up to my room, climbing the stairs as quickly as I could without dislodging Poe from my shoulder and found my father waiting for me.

"Shut the door. We need to talk," Dad said from his seat on the end of my bed, his tone of voice that quiet harshness that parents get when before they really lay into you.

I dropped my bag and did as he asked, already dreading whatever it was he wanted to talk about. Poe let out a soft call, rustling his wings as I transferred him gently to his perch by my desk.

"Ezra, come sit down."

I picked up my bag instead, setting it on my desk and unzipping it open. "I'd rather go ahead and unpack," I said, tossing a bundle of dirty laundry into my hamper. "I might not get a chance to later."

"Erza, you can't go through with this. You can't take the test."

The desperation in my father's voice made me turn around to look at him. "Why not? Because I don't have Talent?" I felt anger boil up in me all over again. Why didn't anyone believe in me? "I know more about the theory of Necromancy than most because I've studied and studied, hoping that something would help trigger my Talent. I may not have the Talent, but I have everything else I need to pass the test. I've got to have a shot, at least." I didn't add the part where all I could think about was saving Avery from marrying into the Ackland family.

"It takes more than just knowing the theory, Ezra! The test is dangerous, and that's not even the point that I'm trying to make here."

"Oh yeah, then why shouldn't I take the test? Why can't I try?"

"Because you aren't my son!" He stared at me as the silence built between us. "You don't have any Talent because you aren't part of the Stanwood bloodline."

I couldn't believe what I was hearing. "What? That's not-"

Dad linked his hands together, studying them without really seeing them. "After your brother was born, there were ...some complications. We went to specialists and tried all we could to have another child, but it just wasn't possible. Your mother was heartbroken."

I was stunned. Reaching back, I rolled my desk chair over to sit. "But then, how am I here?"

He glanced up at me, but his gaze traveled pass me to Poe.

"It was a few nights after Liam's second birthday. A storm came in, and it had been raining hard. I woke up suddenly in the middle of the night to find one of the windows in the bedroom open. Sitting on the sill was a raven. I remember being surprised. Even though the raven is our symbol, we hadn't seen one on the mountain in years.

"An impulse came over me then, that I had to go to the Vault and I had to go quickly. I ran up the path. I wasn't sure what to expect, but when I got to the cemetery, I found it full of ravens. But the oddest part was that Vault stood open."

"That's not possible..." I stuttered. It couldn't be. The Vault was sealed magickally and would only open for a Stanwood, and even then, only for specific occasions. It was like the Vault itself had its own mind. It wouldn't just be open.

"It stood open, and just inside out of the reach of the rain, was a bundle of cloth and a single raven. Even with all the noise from the storm and the ravens, you slept soundly, a raven feather held tightly in your hand. I picked you up, and the raven beside you took a perch on my shoulder when all the others flew off into the storm. He's watched over you ever since."

I looked at Poe, still trying to understand what my father was telling me. I wasn't a Stanwood. I didn't have any Talent because I wasn't a necromancer. My chest grew tight as I fought to control all the emotions raging through me. "How could I just appear in the Vault? It's not possible-"

Dad studied me. "Your mother believes the Great One who guides our family sent you to us. How else is it possible for us to have found you in the Vault? You know as well as I that regular humans aren't able to enter the cemetery without help. And no other Necromancer besides myself or your two-year-old brother could have opened the Vault."

He was right. We were the last- No, they were the last of the Stanwood blood. The war with the Witches had made sure of that. And now, who was I? Did I have another set of parents out there looking for me? I couldn't have just appeared from thin air, right?

"From that moment on, you were our son, and you always will be our son no matter what happens, but..." he paused, searching for the words. "When you didn't develop the signs of Talent, even after all your studying, your mother and I, we never wanted you to feel like you didn't belong. Ezra, we don't want to lose you. The Great Ones may have placed you in our care, but they may not have meant for you to become a Necromancer like us. Even if the Vault opens for you, your chances of passing the test..."

He left the rest unsaid, but I already knew there was a pretty good chance I was facing my death by doing this. So really, what did this change? Avery didn't want me risking my life for her either, but it wasn't more than an hour ago, right here in my room that she told me that I did have Talent. And not to mention Thea, she may have been a little kid still, but her predictions were more powerful than the rest of her family's.

I let out the breath that I'd been holding and leaned forward to put my head in my hands, trying to clear it of all my thoughts. How was it possible that my life could have fallen apart in less than twenty-four hours?

Dad stood and rested a hand on my shoulder. "I can't tell you what to do. You're eighteen now, and this has got to be a decision you make on your own. I just wanted you to know all the information. We never told the Families that you weren't ours. I can explain this to them so that you won't have to take the test."

"No!" I jumped to my feet. "You can't do that. If I don't take the test, then Avery will have to marry Collen. I can't let that happen."

"Ezra," he said, and looked as if he was about to say something else. Instead, he changed his mind and walked over to the door. "Get some rest then, you'll need all of your strength."

He left, and I stared at the closed door for a long time. Everything I'd thought was true about my family, about who I was, just wasn't right anymore. My entire life was built around being a Stanwood Necromancer even though my Talent never manifested. And now? I couldn't even call myself a Stanwood. Maybe Avery was right. I would probably just get myself killed tonight.

I tossed my bag and clothes on the floor because suddenly, unpacking didn't seem all that important. I curled onto my bed instead, pulling the sheet and blankets up around me. Exhaustion pushed on me like a heavyweight, and yet, I couldn't find sleep. There was too much to wrap my head around, and too much pain in my heart.

Poe cawed softly, winging over to walk carefully along the coverlet to settle himself beside me. Peace washed over me, and before I could think otherwise, I drifted off.

Liam woke me late in the afternoon, as the sun sank below the tree line on the mountain. He set a plate of food and a bottle of water down on my desk and left as quietly as he'd come in.

After letting Poe out my little window to find some food for himself, I ate dinner alone in my room, hardly tasting the food. I forced it down, knowing I would need the strength later. Sleeping the little I did had helped, but my mind still spun with the information Dad had told me. If I really wasn't a Stanwood, then why was I found in the Vault? Why would the Great Ones bring me to the Stanwoods?

I closed my eyes, trying to force the never-ending stream of questions out of my mind. I needed to focus on the test. Dad was right. If I wasn't a Stanwood, I really shouldn't take it. What if we went up there, and the Vault refused to open for me? Or worse, it opened, but nothing happened? What could I do then?

It was eight in the evening when I finally went downstairs. Everyone sat in the living room, all but Evelyn and Thea bundled up for the hike to the Vault. They wished me luck before heading up to the spare guest room.

I pulled my heavy jacket out of the hall closet and slipped into it. It still smelled like the herbs in the garden, reminding me of the quiet mornings that I'd go out with mom to look after the plants.

"Are you ready?" Dad asked as came to stand near me in the hall, the others not far behind him.

Nodding, we all turned for the door, stepping out on to the porch and into the freezing night air. We trudged through the newly fallen snow, following the snow-covered, but well-worn, trail to the Stanwood family graveyard. The walk brought back memories of the last time we'd walked as a family out there for Liam's test all those years ago.

I remembered how scared I was back then, fearing that Liam wouldn't come back, or worse, that he wouldn't pass. Anxiety swarmed around inside me, imagining a thousand 'what-ifs.' It was my turn now, and there was an outstanding possibility that I wasn't coming back.

Avery glanced back at me from where she walked ahead, her hair bouncing like threads of moonlight in the darkness. I could do this, I would do this. Avery was my soul mate. I knew that from the countless letters, from the way it felt to hold her in my arms. It didn't matter if she believed in me or not. What mattered was that she was safe and happy. I would do this to ensure that.

We'd reached the gate to the graveyard. The group stopped around me as Father pulled out his keys and unlocked the gate.

Usually, we were the only people out here. Still, the occasional hiker had wandered up here before and triggered the guardian spirits that protected the Vault. To say it didn't end well would be putting it mildly.

We filed in, and Dad locked the gate behind us. There wasn't much difference between the graveyard and the forest behind us. The sky was still partially blocked by the tall trees, the ground was still covered with today's snow. What was different was the way the air felt. Or so Dad and Liam had told me. The air supposedly hummed with the essence of our ancestors and left a tingling feeling along the skin of any Talented that entered our hallowed ground. I couldn't count the number of times I'd walked out here, hoping that I would feel something, anything.

Poe circled the air above us and swooped into land on my shoulder. He shifted, ruffling his feathers in a way that told me he was nervous.

We followed the others to stand in front of the Vault. It was dug into the side of the mountain, showing only the marble front through the bare branches of the bushes that framed it. Everyone turned to me. The eagerness on Nathan's face couldn't have been hidden, and Avery wouldn't look me in the eyes.

Mom clung to me, displacing Poe to one of the bushes so she could sob into my jacket. I hugged her tightly in return. Dad's hand clapped down on my free shoulder.

"I'm proud of you," he said softly, so only I could hear. "You may not have our family's Talent, but your courage, strength, and compassion mark you as one of us."

He pulled Mom away from me, and Liam nodded at me from the back of the group. Poe returned to my shoulder and nipped at my ear.

"Surely, you're not going to allow him to take that bird in with him," Nathan sneered, glancing at my father.

Dad fixed him with a steady gaze. "That bird is a Stanwood familiar, and since this test is Stanwood business, his presence is acceptable. You are here as a witness only, so any further concerns you may have tonight, Nathan, should be kept to yourself."

Nathan crossed his arms against his chest and turned his glare towards me.

Lyssa rolled her eyes and gave me a smile. "Good luck, Ezra."

"Thank you, Ms. Amerson." My voice only shook a little. My heart raced as I walked over to stand in front of the door to the Vault. I could do this. I took a step forward.

"Ezra, wait!" Avery's voice wavered as she stepped out of the group. I turned to see tears glimmering on the edges of her eyes. "I shouldn't have said that earlier. I'm sorry. I-"

I reached out, pulling her into my arms for what I could only hope wasn't the last time.

"Ezra."

The way she spoke my name, it was all I needed to know that she felt the same way about me. I kissed her, there in front of our families, and against all of the traditions. There was more than one gasp that echoed through the night air. Usually, this wouldn't have happened until our bonding ceremony. But, I felt like there were exceptional circumstances on our side tonight.

"You don't have to do this," she whispered.

"I know."

Avery hesitated, I think, because she didn't want to repeat our fight. I waited for her to make up her mind, nervous with everyone's eyes on us.

"Just follow your instinct," she finally said. "You do have power, hidden somewhere in that hard head of yours."

"Ezra, it's time." My father's voice beckoned, and a new

calm fell over me. I may be walking to my death, but I was doing it for Avery. And that was all I needed to know.

Stepping up to the Vault, I glance back at everyone, before I laid my hand on the cold, smooth surface of the door. It warmed instantly at my touch, almost as if the stone itself was alive. It moved, forcing me to step back as it swung open on its own.

A little flood of relief ran through me. One obstacle down, two more to go. I could only dream that they would be as easy.

Forcing one foot after another, I tried not to think about the last time I saw the door open. The inside was pitch black, the only light came from the sliver of moon that shone through the doorway, creating a triangle of light on the floor.

As soon as I cleared the threshold, the door eased shut on its own, leaving me in complete darkness.

My heart pounded in my ears as my eyes fought to see. I turned in a circle, feeling as if the night was closing in on me. What was supposed to happen next?

Poe shifted on my shoulder again, letting out a soft caw.

"Hello?" I called out. My previous thought of the test not trigging came flying back to my mind. I'm Talentless, I'm not even technically a Stanwood. What if I wasn't supposed to be here?

I tried to slow my breathing as the blackness around me closed in. If I couldn't take the test, the door to the Vault wouldn't open on its own until it was time for the next test, or the next member in my family died. I spun around, trying to feel around for anything, a wall, the door.

Pain shattered my panic, forcing me to concentrate on the sharp, sudden bite on my earlobe. Poe squawked loudly.

Reaching up, I felt for his feathers, gently laying a hand on him. "Thanks, partner."

Poe had cleared my mind enough for logic to take over. The door had opened for me. It recognized me. That had to mean it would give me the test- The bird cawed softly, then launched himself into the air.

"Wait, POE!" Fear gripped me all over again. How could he see to fly in here? What if he hit a wall or the ceiling and hurt himself?

Light flooded the space, blinding me. Spots danced in front of my eyes. The sound of rustling cloth reached my ears, but I hadn't moved.

"Who's there?!" I forced my eyes open, trying to see past the glaring white that had replaced the darkness. A figure stood before me. I focused on him, willing my eyes to adjust faster. "Who are you?"

The man was haggard-looking with an unkempt beard and long raven black hair to match. He wore a black suit, a black duster coat. Even his eyes were black.

"Who are you?" I asked again, a little louder.

He shrugged. "Who I am isn't important here."

I stared back at him. "What's important, then?"

"Who are you?"

This had to be a joke. I turned for the door - and it wasn't there. Unbroken white space surrounded me. I spun around to the guy, but he was gone as well.

My heart started pounding in my ears again. I forced myself to take deep breaths. There was nothing but white around me.

"Who are you?" The man's voice repeated, echoing as he appeared in front of me again.

"I'm Ezra."

"You are the *adopted* son of William Stanwood." He smiled at me, and it wasn't a nice one.

My stomach dropped. "How do you know that?"

"I know a lot of things."

His matter-of-fact tone was really starting to piss me off, and on top of everything else, he wasn't answering my questions. The man before me shifted his stance, the set of his shoulders squaring a bit more. It was almost as if he'd read my thoughts.

"The young Manser girls are right. You do have Talent."

His words hit me with what felt like a physical blow. "How do you -"

He tilted his head at me like a curious bird inspecting its morning meal.

"Right, you know everything." I glanced around, the glaring white space was still harsh on my eyes. I couldn't see Poe anywhere. "How do I even know that I can trust you?"

"You don't have to trust me, but you do have to learn to trust yourself," he said, taking a step closer. He reached into his pocket and pulled out a silvery length of chain. He held out his closed fist to me, the chain dangling. "The reason your Talent has yet to manifest is because you've not had the proper tools nor the right training."

I didn't understand. "But I've studied everything my family has, I've spent countless hours trying-"

"Ezra, your power is not the same as the Stanwood's. The Great Ones have allowed me to help guide you through the difficult times ahead as there is no one else left to do so."

"Wait, what? What difficult times? I don't know who you are or whether to believe any of this."

He turned his hand over, revealing a pendant with a swirl of five lines that met a red stone in its center. He pressed his palm closer, urging me to take it. "That's not important right now. What is important is that you pass your test. This will help you reach the end of the path the Great Ones have set you on-"

A gong sounded, loud enough that I could feel the vibrations along my skin.

"What was that?"

The man in front of me looked grim, scared even. "Our

time is up. I can not stall the test any longer." He shoved the pendant into my hand.

Turning, he ran away from me, his duster coat flapping wildly behind him in a non-existent wind. The man jumped into the air, his form twisting until a bird emerged from the tangle of cloth. Poe glided through the air, and all I could do was stare at him.

I'd just spoken with him.

He wheeled around, coming to land on my shoulder once more. I'd known he was special, but I had the sneaking suspicion that I still hadn't seen all he could do yet.

"You're more than a familiar, aren't you?" I said, reaching up to smooth some of his feathers down. It was like the founding story, the raven coming to guide the first Stanwood to the Vault, to offer him access to the power that he'd had inside of him all along. But if I wasn't a Stanwood, what was I?

I felt like my head was going to implode. There was too much to try to take in and process. I wasn't a Stanwood, but I was still a Necromancer. I did have power, I could do something, but what exactly?

I looked down at the pendant in my hand. The swirling design was familiar, but I couldn't place where I'd seen it before.

Poe nibbled gently on my earlobe, then turned his attention to our right. A portal stood by itself in the whiteness. It's silvery surface reflecting light into the room.

The bird shifted on my shoulder, and I craned my neck to look at him. He took off, flying through the portal. I guess I was supposed to go through it, too. I followed with a silent prayer that I would make it through this alive. For Avery, and for myself.

Chapter 3

A cold hand was wrapped around my own. That was the first thing I noticed. The second was how much I hurt. Everywhere.

I opened my eyes, thankful that it was dark, but confused when I found myself staring up at the ceiling of my own room. My body felt too hot, stifling under the blankets that were piled on top of me.

"Ezra?" Mom's voice was just a whisper from the foot of my bed, but her eyes were bright with relief when I looked down at her. She clutched at the footboard, trying hard to stay quiet.

"Mom," I said, my voice weak. "What happened?"

Avery stirred next to me. She was sitting in my desk chair and had slumped over the side of the bed, asleep. It was her hand that was wrapped around my own. She opened her eyes, and they reminded me of something. Something that had happened.

"Your test, it took too long, the others began to think..." Mom paused a brief moment, then forced herself to continue. "That maybe you didn't make it. But then after dawn yesterday, the door opened, and you were lying inside, and Poe was there, too." The bird cawed softly into the darkness from his perch. She wiped the tears from her face. "Ezra, you passed! You passed the test! Aren't you happy?"

It came back to me then in a rush of memory and emotions. How was I supposed to tell them?

"Ezra?" Avery's soft voice drifted to me. "What's wrong?"

I shook my head, trying to form the right words in my mind. I pushed myself up, only to collapse against the headboard. I didn't have any strength, but this was important. "I need to talk to Dad."

"You need to rest," Avery said. "You've been through a lot, and you're feverish still."

"No, that's," I paused, I couldn't tell them yet. Dad needed to hear it first, then the other Heads of the Families. "I need to talk to Dad. It's important." I tried to put strength into my voice, that forceful insistence that I'd heard Dad use so often with others to get his point across.

"Lay back down," Mom said, patting the blanket over my foot. "I'll go get your father and something for you to eat. You look practically starved."

I wasn't hungry, but I didn't argue with her. She left Avery and me alone in my room, shutting the door softly behind her.

"I told you, didn't I?" Avery said with a smile when we were finally alone. "I knew you had the Stanwood gift in you somewhere."

"My Talent isn't Revival."

Her smile faded. "What? How's that possible. You're a Stanwood, you-"

I looked up at Poe on his perch. He regarded me with a quiet stare.

"I'm not really a Stanwood either. Gods, Avery, everything is so messed up."

Avery regarded me with a skeptical look like maybe I

talking in my sleep. "Ezra, what are you talking about?" She looked at her hands. "You aren't making any sense. Of course, you're a Stanwood."

Dad chose that moment to knock on the door and enter. Nathan and Lyssa filed in behind him.

"It's good to see you awake," Lyssa said.

Nathan glared daggers at me. Guess he wasn't too happy that I'd survived. I pushed myself up straighter, gathering myself for what I had to say. "I was just about to tell Avery what happened."

"You know that it is forbidden to talk about your test," Nathan snapped at me.

"I don't want to talk about the test, exactly," I said quietly. "I want to talk about how the Necromantic Circle has five families again."

Everyone stared at me with unease. Finally, my father cleared his throat. "Ezra, you've been through a lot. We should let you rest and - "

Poe screeched, interrupting my father with a few shakes of his wings, which shook the pendent free from his talon's grasp. It swung freely from his perch, where the chain had become tangled.

Nathan, who stood closest, stepped back, putting as much distance between himself and the pendant as he possibly could without leaving the room.

Dad and Lyssa shared a grim look.

"What's that?" Avery asked.

"It was given to me before my test started. I think it helped me - with my Talent."

"That's impossible," Nathan whispered. "That necklace has been lost for years, and you just happened to find it in the Vault?" He turned on my father. "What else have you been hiding from us, Stanwood?"

"I didn't find it!" I yelled before Dad even had a chance to say anything in his defense. "I said it was given to me."

"And who, pray tell, was in the Vault with you?"

"Poe," I glanced at the raven on his perch. "He told me that Avery and Thea were right, that there was a power in me, but it was different from the rest of the Stanwood Family. Then he gave me that," I pointed to the pendent, "and said that he was here to help guide me through the difficult times ahead. And that was before the test started."

Lyssa shared another look with my father. "This wasn't normal," she said. "In this case, we need to hear what happened."

Even Nathan agreed grimly.

"Alright, Ezra," Dad said, "tell us everything that happened."

I *followed Poe through the silvery portal. The heat hit me immediately. I strained to see the tops of the trees that stood like giants around me. I was in a jungle, but where?*

Poe was perched on a bush not far to my left. His dark feathers standing out like a thorn against its bright flowers.

"There you are!"

I whipped around to see a girl, tiny and delicate, stepping out of the undergrowth with a spear. She wore a wrap of bright orange, like a monk's almost. But even though the color was vibrant, her expression of suppressed fear and urgency was what really startled me.

"You're talking to me?" I asked her, looking around.

She nodded. "Come, my people need you." She motioned for me to follow her, and even took my hand when I hesitated, dragging me forward. "Come, Come!"

I followed the girl as she ran barefoot through the jungle, barely able to keep up with her. Poe glided over us, never too far from my sight. We came around a large root of the tree on a crest of a hill, and I saw, in the low valley that lay ahead, a village of huts with thatched roofs.

The girl ran towards it, dodging hollows and tree roots like she'd been running on this land since the day she was born.

I panted behind her, already drenched in sweat from my layers of winter clothing. "Hey, wait up!"

"Hurry!" she yelled, but she did slow her pace a fraction.

Stumbling into the village, I couldn't see another soul in sight. I caught up with the girl in an open space surrounded by the little mud huts, only to find her facing a creature twice her size. I froze, even though every instinct was telling me to turn around and run. The creature looked like a giant dog, or maybe it had been one at some point. Its double tail whipped back and forth in anger as it growled at us.

Poe screeched overhead, diving at it from the air as the girl tried to attack with her spear. The beast snarled at her, dodging away.

My feet felt rooted to the ground as I scanned the forest around us, looking for anything or anyone that might be able to help us. I was out of luck.

What was I supposed to do? I'd never seen a creature like this. I'd hadn't even read about anything like it in all my studies. It definitely wasn't a normal dog.

I shook my head and fought to keep my breathing even. I wasn't prepared for this.

Poe screamed again, this time flying towards me. The girl and beast circled, looking for weakness in each other. Her attention shifted to me for a fraction of a second, and the creature lunged for her. It pushed her to the ground.

"No!" I ran towards them, not even sure what I was going to do when I got there. I tackled the beast, drawing its attention from the girl. It snapped its enormous teeth at me before closing its jaw around my arm. My heavy jacket offered little protection from the razor-like canines. I struggled with it, screaming in pain as I felt each tooth sink into my skin.

"Versay Kalum Jah!" I don't know what prompted me to yell it. The words were as foreign as the creature attacking me. The phrase had formed in my mind, and the Talent Avery and Poe both said I had, caught and held fast to the words. The sensation was like nothing I'd ever felt before. The feeling of warmth flowed from the depths of my heart, burning veins as it spilled out of my outstretched hand.

The beast flew off me as if it had been knocked back with the blast of a grenade. All I could do was stare at my wounded arm through the shredded remains of my coat.

That had been nothing like what Liam had described his Talent to feel like. He'd always told me the Stanwood power was cold. The type of energy that breathed fresh life into the dead. Nothing about our work was 'hot.'

A growl echoed out through the clearing and brought my head up to see the beast was standing. I forced myself to my feet and faced it. The pendant Poe had given me heavy in my hand.

Poe landed on my shoulder, and this time, I could feel him. I don't mean the feeling of his talons on my shoulder, but his essence, his magic. Where I'd felt my Talent to be warm like the heat of an oven, his was what I imagined stepping into hell might be like. The intensity of it radiated against my skin, adding to the humidity that already pressed against me.

The beast charged us, rushing towards us with a speed that wasn't natural. Poe flew off as words formed in my mind once again. "Eklam sou vesital. Shetal losse felit." Talent burned along my skin, and I watched as it flowed out of my hand and blossom over the beast, encasing it in a hard glass looking prism mid-stride.

I fell to my knees, any strength I had gone. All the reading and studying about Talent I'd done growing up hadn't prepared me for actually using it. Poe landed next to me and began tapping at the metal pendant in my hand. He looked up at me with expectant eyes.

"What?" I gasped, still out of breath.

He snatched the necklace from me and flew over to the beast, carefully landing a foot or so away. Poe walked over the uneven ground until he could reach out with the pendant and touch the glassy prism encasing the beast. The glass shattered in a whirlwind of shards that swirled tornado-like into the stone of the pendant.

Poe stood still until it was over, then he flew back to me, returning the necklace to my hand.

Gripping at the trunk of a nearby tree, I used it to pull myself up inch by inch until I was standing on my own feet again. The girl was still lying on the ground where the beast had tackled her, partially covered by blood-splattered foliage. I mustered up the last of my strength and went to her, hoping that I wasn't too late. Praying that she was just unconscious.

I was wrong. My feet slid out from under me. I'd hesitated, and she'd died. It was my fault she was dead. I glanced around at the empty huts of the village. How was I supposed to tell her family, her parents, that I'd let her die? That I'd failed to keep her safe. How was I supposed to tell my family I'd failed my test?

Sitting there in the heat, I watched over her as the sun dipped low into the horizon, and the only way I could tell was by the color and the angle at which it filtered through the trees. Even Poe left me after a while. All I could do was stare at her.

"Hassim?"

The word was jarring after only hearing the sounds of the jungle for so long. I looked up into the face of the old man who stood near me. He wore a robe similar to that of the girl's, only difference being that it was edged in red.

"I'm sorry," I said in a rush. "I'm so sorry. I didn't - I couldn't save her."

He glanced over at the girl with heavy, tear-rimmed eyes. "We can not save all, Hassim."

"But if I'd only known!" I yelled, stumbling to my feet. "I could have saved her if I'd just-"

He held up his hands, trying to steady me. "Easy, you are ill..."

Black flooded my vision, and I felt myself fall, but I don't remember hitting the earth.

I told them everything, not holding back anything more other than the fact that Poe had changed his form. The Heads of all the Families shared another look in the silence that followed. It only made me more nervous. They knew now that I'd failed, that I hadn't saved the girl-

"He described the lost family's power perfectly," Lyssa said, looking to my father. "Could it really be possible that your son was chosen to revive the Reinhardt line?"

"How do we know he isn't making all of this up?" Nathan argued.

Lyssa stepped in front of him before I even had a chance to speak. "You were in diapers when the last of the Reinhardts were killed. How do you know he's lying? You forget that the Emersons worked closely with our lost brothers and sisters. I saw their powers first hand. And that description Ezra just gave was to the T."

Nathan's gaze iced over as he held his ground. "I must see this to believe it."

Dad studied the two of them before turning to me. "I hate to ask when you're still recovering, but we must witness your Talent first hand. If it's true that you are the new founder of the Reinhardt line, we must confirm it."

They wouldn't believe me until they saw it. Great. Let's just hope I could figure out how to do *something* with my new Talent.

Avery helped me stand. Someone had changed me into a set of flannel PJs at some point. I didn't even want to think about how that had happened. I slipped my feet into a pair of slippers as Nathan and Lyssa headed down the stairs ahead of us. Pausing for a moment, I began to untangle the pendant's chain from Poe's perch. He stirred as I pulled the chain away and flapped up to perch on my shoulder.

With Dad and Avery to keep me steady, we somehow made

it downstairs to the living room in one piece. Avery's mother and sister sat on the couch, my brother waited near the fireplace with Nathan's son, Collen. I wondered when he'd arrived, though, knowing Nathan, it was probably about five minutes after I started my Test.

"William!" Mom shrieked. She stood in the doorway we'd just passed through, a tray of food held in her hands. "What is he doing out of bed-"

"I'm okay, Mom," I insisted.

"You certainly don't look okay!"

"It's important," Dad said with a pained look. "We'll have him back in bed soon."

Nathan motioned around himself. "Is this enough room? Or should we perhaps step outside?"

"I don't even know what you want me to do," I said, "I'm not sure I could-"

"Oh, come now." Nathan stared at me. "Surely, if you're going to claim that you're going to start a new family line, you should have something of merit to back up your claim."

Shock filtered around the room.

"He didn't claim anything like that, Nathan," my father said with a dangerous edge to his voice.

"He might as well have. Just how are we to know that he's telling the truth? How do we know that you haven't just been hiding the most powerful Necromantic artifact from us for all these years?"

I glanced at the pendant. "You know what this is?"

Nathan glared at me. "Boy, that is the pendant the Head of the Reinhardt Family wore. The pendant that was lost years ago when the Circle fought against the Witches in Salem, and most of the Reinhardt family was killed."

I remembered that story, Dad had told me about that battle only a month or two before I'd headed off to college, as a warning. He wanted me to know why it was so dangerous for Necromancers out in the world, even if I didn't have Talent.

But now what happened in the jungle made a little more sense. The Reinhardts were Summoners.

"They were the family that summoned beasts, demons to fight," I said, staring down at the pendant.

If I'm supposed to be able to summon creatures, why couldn't I have done that back in the jungle? I only fought a beast, I didn't summon it.

"So, let's see this new power of yours," Nathan sneered at me.

I glanced around at my family. Liam actually looked a little scared. Mom had set down her tray and now stood next to my father. My eyes finally rested on Avery, and she gave me a soft smile.

I thought back to all the exercises I'd done as a child, and what little I knew about the Reinhardt. I focused on the pendant again, and mentally searched for the warmth, that heat that had burned my veins. My Talent flared to life in the depths of my chest, forcing me to gasp at the sudden intensity of it. I fell to my knees.

"Ezra!"

I heard my mom shout, but it was all I could do to keep the power contained within me, and you know, not kill myself in the process. Two little slippered feet appeared in my line of vision as I stared at the carpet. Glancing up, I found Thea standing there, her lithe frame barely taller than my hunched form. She reached out, her too cold fingers lightly touching my forehead.

A chill swept through me, cooling the fire that raged in my body to a manageable heat. I opened my eyes, unaware that I'd even closed them. "Thanks," I said.

"It'll take time to learn control, but I see what will be. You will master it." Thea's voice chimed almost like a bell.

"Enough stalling, let's see this power of yours," Nathan snapped.

I stood again, letting Dad steady me when I swayed a little on my feet. I was a Necromancer. I was a Summoner. I could do this, and I would.

I clutched the pendant tightly in my hand and focused my attention on the bare spot in the center of the room. Thea had cooled enough of my Talent that I could call just enough forward for what I needed. But as weak as I was now, and using more Talent would only make me feel worse. And quickly. I just needed to focus forward and get this done.

The words I needed sprang to my mind just as they had back in the jungle. I honestly had no clue what I was saying. I only knew the meaning behind it, the goal I wanted to achieve.

"*Vershala tulian das lo berruas. Kalha vas notha rak!*"

I screamed the last word of the spell with the very last of my strength, pushing my Talent to hold fast to the phrases. I felt the power burn, just like it had before, searing my veins with power.

An intricate circle appeared on the floor, contrasting with the floral print of the carpet with a violent red glow as it spun and pulsed along with the rapid beating of my heart. One last word came to mind, one word I had to call out to finish the summoning.

"*Kastem!*" The name rolled through me like a train, dragging every last ounce of energy from my body as I collapsed to the ground again. The circle shrank suddenly to a pinpoint on the carpet and exploded in a flash of light.

I shielded my eyes from it, but even as the bright white burned, I could see the silhouette of the beast materializing where the circle had been.

Nathan stumbled back, sinking into an overstuffed armchair when his feet hit it. "I can't believe it."

Dad knelt next to me, his hand a solid weight on my shoulder. After a moment, he helped me stand, this time holding me upright so that I didn't fall again.

Avery quickly took up her post at my free side, smiling up at me with her bright blue eyes. "I knew you could do it."

The beast stared at me from across the room, an expectant gaze that chilled the fiery burn in my veins. I was a Summoner. I had control over the beast now, but I knew that every time I called it forth from the depths of whatever prison my pendant held, I would remember the girl I failed to save.

"I can't save everyone..." I mumbled, repeating the old man's words to myself. Glancing around the room at my family, and the other Heads of the Necromantic Circle, I feared for the future. How many of them would I fail to save as well? Nathan and I exchanged a not-so-pleasant look, and I stared him down until he finally broke and looked away.

"Avery will be the next Head of the Manser family," I said. "And she will be so without a bond if she so chooses. We have far more important business to deal with now than sticking our noses into the way other families conduct their lives."

Lyssa nodded in agreement. "You warned us earlier that there are hard times ahead of us. We need to focus on preparing and readying ourselves for whatever may come in the future."

"But the Manser family will need successors, especially if we're on the verge of trouble!" Nathan shouted, jumping to his feet.

Thea turned to him. "We Mansers can see what is, what will be, and what has been. We can control our own fate. There will be plenty of successors to our family name, but not before we see these troubled times through."

"You are a child-" Nathan spat.

"I will remind you one last time, that 'child' is the most powerful Seer to be born since our founding Mother," Avery said in a low, threatening voice. "I ask you as one Head of a Family to another, to speak to her with respect."

Nathan stared at us all for a long time before squaring his shoulders. "Collen, gather our things. It's time we returned home."

Nathan and Collen left quickly, not wasting a minute, as I focused on figuring out how to un-summon the demon in my parent's living room. It took a little trial and error, and a lot of guidance from Thea before I was able to send the beast back to wherever it had come from.

Avery and my father helped me back to bed afterward, and I sank gratefully into the sheets.

"You should get some rest," my father said. "I'll see what information can be gathered, and we'll talk again once you're feeling up to it."

He left Avery and me alone, shutting the door behind him.

Sleep pulled at my eyes, but I forced them wide in a futile attempt to stay awake. "Avery, I ..."

"I know," she said, leaning down to kiss my forehead. "You'll stand with me, right? At the ceremony?"

"Of course." I closed my eyes at the feeling of her lips, and I couldn't find the strength to open them again as sleep claimed me.

Chapter 4

I stayed in bed for nearly a week, focusing on resting. I talked to Poe once we were alone, but he acted as he always had, like a bird. It got to the point where I wondered if I'd just imagined him as a human. Maybe I'd even imagined it all. But the pendant I wore told me differently, and I could feel the Talent pulse along my skin, spreading like a burning rash.

"Are you sure you feel alright?" Mom asked for about the billionth time while I shrugged on my coat. I'd considered leaving it behind but settled for keeping it unzipped. Sweat beaded on my forehead, and I wiped it away impatiently.

"I'm fine," I groaned, ignoring the slight tremble in my hand as I reached for the door handle. Okay, so I wasn't a hundred percent, but if I had to listen to her fawn over me all day *again*, I was going to scream; in that girly, horror film kinda way.

Mom followed me to the porch to wish Avery and her family a safe trip. Lyssa had left shortly after Nathan, but Avery had stuck around a little longer so our families could start on plans.

The snow glare was bright and hurt my eyes, but the cold

air felt fantastic. Out in the driveway, Dad was loading the last of the Manser's luggage into the back of their car. Mom passed Avery on the small porch as she went to say goodbye to Evelyn.

Wobbly on my feet, I clutched at the door frame and tried to play it cool. Concern filled Avery's eyes as she stepped up to me. Crap, guess I hadn't been as smooth as I'd hoped.

"I don't want to leave yet, not until I know you're feeling better..." Avery said, picking at the knit pair of gloves she held.

"What do you mean? I'm fine." I forced myself to stand steady, letting go of the frame with a prayer that I wouldn't fall on my face.

She leveled a stern gaze at me. "Completely back to your old self?"

"Well, that may be a few more days yet." I smiled weakly at her. "Besides, you have to start preparing for your ceremony."

Avery hesitated, looking away. "I still can't believe this is happening so fast. I thought we'd have more time to adjust before..."

I took her hands into mine. "We'll work it out. The Heads are asking for our bond. We don't have to do anything you're not ready for or uncomfortable with." To be honest, I wasn't sure what I was comfortable with yet. Going from not having any hope I could marry another necromancer to actually preparing for the ceremony, left me with a bad sense of whiplash.

Avery smiled softly, her blue eyes glowing in the morning light. "Alright, but you better promise to take care of yourself. I can't have you standing at the altar half dead."

"Promise," I said.

She stepped closer and wrapped her arms around me. I returned her hug.

"I'll see you soon, in just a few weeks."

"You better write," she whispered.

"Wouldn't dream of doing anything else."

She left me standing on the porch as I watched her climb into the car and wave from the window.

Dad and Mom come up the steps, turning as the Manser's car started down the narrow roads of our mountain. I gave one last wave to Avery as she twisted in her seat to look back at me.

"Ezra, come back inside and rest. I'll make you some breakfast." Mom tried to shoo me back into the house, but I sidestepped her, taking careful steps down off the porch.

"I'll be back in a little bit. I just want to take a walk."

Her lips pursed in a way that I knew from experience that she was thinking about arguing with me.

Dad saved me, placing a gentle hand on her shoulder. "At least take Poe with you..."

"Already planning on it," I called back as Poe flew off from his perch on the gutter overhead.

I knew exactly where I wanted to go, but it took me a while to walk up to the Vault. Some of the snow had melted, exposing brown patches of frozen earth that I had plenty of time to study each time I paused to catch my breath. I peeled off my coat as the heat under my skin nearly made me faint. Poe stayed close the entire walk but flew off once the gate to the cemetery was in sight.

The Vault's door stood open as if waiting for me. The sight of it made me pause. I glanced around, looking to see if Liam was about, but the cemetery was empty save for myself. I walked closer, pausing in the Vault's doorway to look in.

In the center of the room, a stone bench looked like it had grown right out of the marble floor. That wasn't there before, was it? Poe perched there, shifting his feathers. Taking a hesitant step inside, I found that the door to the Vault stayed opened, leaving weak, winter sunlight to fill the cavernous room.

I took a seat, dropping my coat on the ground next to me before heaving a sigh. "Maybe I wasn't so ready for that walk."

Poe cawed and took flight. I watched as his shape twisted in mid-air, landing just feet from me. Just like he did a week ago.

"Why don't you stay, human?" I asked, realizing it must be troublesome at the very least to live as a bird. "Are you human?"

He blinked at me, tilting his head to the side. "I can't maintain this form outside the Vault. This place is different from the rest of the world outside. It's part of the same Half-world that you took your test in. It's a place that stands between that world, " he pointed outside, "and the world of the Great Ones, which you return to when you pass on."

"So, you're a spirit, then? A ghost?" I don't know if the walk left me confused, but that didn't seem right.

"Something like that." He took a seat next to me on the bench. "How are you feeling?"

I fought not to roll my eyes. Like I hadn't heard that question enough lately. "I'm-" I almost said ' fine,' but the stern look Poe gave me stopped the white lie. I shrugged. "I'm not completely better, but if I sit in that house doing nothing for another week, I'll lose my mind."

Poe chuckled. "Then we will start your training, but slowly. I don't want you to end up back in a sickbed."

"I wanted to ask you..." I hesitated. The question had been eating away at me since Dad first told the story of finding me here in this very Vault with Poe as a baby. Now that he could answer me...

"Of course." His tone was expectant. It made me wonder if I was that transparent.

"Where did you find me? What about my birth parents? Are they-" I stopped as his expression grew guarded. Even before he could answer me, I knew the truth. "They're gone?"

"I'm sorry," he said softly.

To learn that my mom and dad weren't my real parents, then to learn that my biological parents were already gone before I knew them. I felt cheated. "How did it happen? Why bring me here? Who-" I stopped myself. There were too many questions in my mind, each seeming just as important as the last.

Poe gave me a softer look, an expression that didn't match well the unkempt beard and hardened lines of his face.

"It is not like you were randomly selected for this, Ezra. Your grandparents on your father's side were Reinhardt and Stanwood. And though your father was a true Talentless necromancer, that didn't stop the Witches from hunting him down."

So that was why the Vault still responded to me. I had just enough of the Stanwood blood to activate it. "And my mother?"

"She was normal. She didn't even know the Family secret."

I closed my eyes. I didn't want to ask, but I needed to know the truth. "How did they die?"

Poe was silent a moment before speaking softly, "The Witches found them together. Your father was driving, and they caused an accident. Your mother was badly injured and was taken to the hospital. You were born shortly before she died."

Silence hung between us as I fought to understand it all.

"How do you know all this?" I glanced out the open door, looking at the gravestones of previous Stanwoods. It made me wonder if my real parents had a grave somewhere out there.

Poe went so quiet and still that I had to turn to see if he was still sitting next to me.

"I have watched over the Necromancers a long time. And this war against the Witches has gone on long enough. When you were brought into this world, I not only saw that you possessed the Reinhardt Talent but also, that you would have a power like no other Reinhardt that has come before you. I went to the Great Ones and pleaded to them. I begged them to grant me a form in your world so I might guide you in putting an end to the senseless killing."

Staring at him, I felt my hands shake. End the war between the Necromancers and Witches? "But, they killed my birth parents," I said. The anger burned slow, raising in me something I didn't recognize. "They've killed thousands of Necromancers across the world. They killed off the whole Reinhardt line!"

"Not the whole line," he said patiently. "What do you want? Revenge for your parent's deaths? Are you willing to orphan yet another, to put another child in your position? It'll only perpetuate the cycle. It has to end somewhere, Ezra."

My nails bit into my palms as I clenched and unclenched my hands. I could see Poe's reasoning, I even understood it. But what I felt was a whole other matter. I got that the war was terrible, but someone had to pay for the crimes committed against my parents and me, against the other necromancers.

Poe sighed. "Let us put this discussion aside for another time. We have a more important task in front of us."

I sat back down, fighting the dizziness threatening to topple me over. "Okay," I said, unsure. "What's that?"

"I must teach you to use that Talent of yours, then I'll teach you how to fight."

"Wait, I thought you wanted to end the war?" I asked.

"I do, but if you could end a war with just words, Ezra, there wouldn't be any wars to end. You also have to survive long enough to speak." He stood, only to take a few steps before sinking to the floor, sitting tailor style in front of me. "Let's start with meditation, then we'll discuss the theory behind the Reinhardt Talent."

"But I already know how to meditate." I'd learned all that back as a child, while still waiting for my Talent would emerge.

"And when was the last time you actually practiced?" Poe asked with a knowing look.

He caught me there. "It's been a year or two," I hedged. I

think I'd stopped about when I'd given up hope on ever finding my Talent and started researching other options for my life.

"Meditation is vital to mastering the summoner's Talent. Without a disciplined mind, you can't hope to control the beasts you call, much less your own power. Reinhardt children learn to meditate before they even know that is what they are doing."

I took a deep breath and slid off the bench, copying Poe's posture. My hands rested lightly in my lap.

"Let go and clear your mind," Poe said, his voice sinking low.

Even though it had been some time since I'd last meditated, the practice came back quickly. I took another deep breath and closed my eyes. My mind cleared on its own, it was kinda like riding a bike in that way. But keeping the stray thoughts at bay took effort. I had a lot of work ahead of me.

———

For two weeks, I walked up to the Vault every day to study with Poe. We concentrated on meditation until my strength fully returned, and then, slowly, I started working on accessing my Talent. The power had built up in my body over the weeks since my test. To the point my temperature hovered around 105 and I wore t-shirts on my walks as the snow continued to fall on the mountain.

Mom fretted at first, thinking I was going to catch my death, but after a while, she left me alone. I didn't talk about what I did up there, only mentioning I was trying to figure out how my Talent worked. That seemed enough for them to leave me be. Things between my 'parents' and I had been different since my test, and no one wanted to bring up the herd of elephants that had stampeded into the room.

For physical training, Poe started with basic fighting

stances. Some of which I'd already known from my training with Dad and Liam. Necromancy used to be just about using Talent, but with enemies like the Witches out there now, you had to know how to defend yourself as well.

"Like this," Poe said, repositioning my hand. "Faster now."

I stepped through the sequence of moves he'd taught me again, sending a steady stream of punches and kicks his way.

"Now, summon your beast," he said, blocking my attacks.

I bit down my panic. I'd been practicing summoning since we'd started training in earnest, but I'd never tried to do it *while* I was fighting.

Poe threw a punch back at me, and I blocked it, sidestepping out of the way as I concentrated on my power.

"*Vershala tulian das lo berruas.*" I started the spell, but as I turned to block another attack, I caught movement in the doorway of the Vault.

"Ezra!" Dad's voice echoed through the stone interior as he rushed in. I could feel his own power building, like a cold breeze through the heat as it reached out to the graveyard.

Braking away from Poe, I frantically planted myself between them facing Dad. "No, wait!"

I tried to drop my own power, releasing it before I'd finished the spell. Pain shot through my mind, forcing me to my knees. It felt like a thousand needles were pushing their way through my skull.

"What did you do to him?" Dad rushed past to grab hold of Poe, slamming him up against the wall.

"I did nothing," Poe said simply.

"Dad, let him go!" I stood on weak legs, trying to keep my balance. The pain blurred my vision. "It's not what you think."

"Not what I think?" He didn't take his eyes off Poe "I come up here and find you're being attacked by a stranger in the Vault! Who are you? How'd you even get in here?"

"Dad!" I yelled, taking a step forward, but decided against

more movement. The room was spinning too fast. "That's Poe."

He and Poe stared at each other for a long moment before Dad stepped away, releasing him.

I let myself sink back to the floor, unable to stand on my own.

"Ezra, are you alright?" Dad asked, still refusing to take his eyes off Poe.

"It's a reaction headache. Ezra has too much Talent built up," Poe said. I could feel his eyes studying me, calculating.

"I'm fine," I said, attempting to stand again. The last thing I wanted to do was be forced to 'rest.' I wobbled on my feet and caught Dad's arm as he reached out to me.

"Meditate tonight, and practice those exercises I taught you. They will help you ease the pain. We will continue tomorrow."

I nodded, ignoring Dad's gaze as he watched us. Poe gave a nod of his own to Dad. "Mr. Stanwood."

He took off, running a few steps before jumping into the air. Poe's form shifted until the black raven came circling around. He did a pass, then flew out into the night. Coward.

"Why didn't you tell me about Poe?" Dad asked, releasing my arm once I was steady on my feet. "That he could-"

"What, like you told me I was adopted?" I turned away from him, heading for the door of the Vault. By the time I got there, I had to grab the edge of the stone to keep from falling. The pain blurred my vision and made me feel as if I was trying to walk on a ship in the middle of a hurricane

Dad came up beside me, looping one of my arms around his neck for support.

"Here, hang on to me," he said.

As much as I hated not leaving the Vault on my own, I did as I was told, grabbing hold of his jacket as he wrapped an arm around my back. The Vault door closed silently behind us after we'd left.

Dad and I walked in silence as we started down the mountain, and the last words I'd snapped to him echoed in my mind. I regretted saying them, but there wasn't any way to take them back now. I wasn't sure I wanted to. Just because I regretted them, didn't mean they weren't true.

By the time Dad was helping me up the front steps to the house, I was starting to feel a little better. Like only a hundred needles were pressing into my head.

The screen door slammed behind us, and mom came out of the kitchen, drying her hands on a dishtowel.

"There you two are..." She stopped, taking in my prone state. "What happened?"

Dad helped me through to the living room. "He just wore himself out. No need to fuss."

"I'll fuss as much as I want to," she snapped back and turned to me. "Don't you move, I'll be right back with something for you to eat." She disappeared back into the kitchen, and I looked up from where he'd dropped me on the couch.

"I just want to sleep," I moaned.

Dad sat in his recliner, reaching for his newspaper. "I believe Poe gave you homework to do, and it wouldn't hurt to humor your mother right now."

"She's not my mother," I mumbled, throwing my head back against the couch.

"Excuse me?" Dad said in a dangerous tone. "I must not have heard you right."

I sat up straight, sick of the pretending. "She's not my mother. You aren't my real parents!"

"I'm going to tell you this once." His voice was quiet as he set his paper down. "We might not be your birth parents, but ever since I found you, we've treated you just like one of our own. We didn't know if you'd be a Necromancer and maybe we should have told you that sooner, but there was nothing we haven't done for you that we didn't think was in your best interest."

I pulled myself to my feet and left without another word to him. Why did they have to wait until I was about to take the test to tell me? What if I had turned out to be normal? All that studying, all that time learning about necromancy, would have been wasted.

I passed mom in the hallway.

"What about your dinner?" she said, holding the plate of food in her hands.

"Thanks, but I'm not hungry."

I tried not to notice how red her eyes looked or how she frowned up at me as I turned to climb the stairs.

Safe in my room, I sat on the edge of my bed, wishing the world would stop spinning. I thought of the lessons Poe had taught me. I held up my hand, focusing my will on my outstretched palm. Red energy formed, sparking between my fingers. I willed it into a shape, forcing the power into a ball of crackling red light. Sweat broke out across my forehead, and I sighed, releasing the energy. It vanished in a wisp of smoke. My skin didn't feel quite as hot, the room didn't sway as much as it did as when I walked into it. With a sigh, I pulled my legs up onto the bed and stretched out.

Why didn't they tell me?

I held up my hand toward the ceiling and started the exercise again.

The next week was mind-numbingly slow, but the time to leave for Avery's ceremony finally came. I packed lightly. A few changes of clothes and, almost as an afterthought, my cell-phone. I wasn't sure it'd be useful, but it'd never hurt to carry it. Dad and I set out a day or two before Mom and Liam. Mom had wanted to finish setting up the greenhouses for our week-long trip away, and Liam had offered to stay and help her.

Dad, Poe, and I loaded up into my SUV and drove south as the sun rose up over the mountains. I drove first, taking us out of the Blue Ridge Mountains and into Gastonia, where we stopped briefly before Dad took over driving for a bit.

I felt anxious and nervous at the same time because, after the bonding ceremony, Avery and I would be as good as married in the eyes of our Families. And since now Avery was Head of the Manser Family, I was afraid the whole celebration was going to be a showy production. I'd been to a bonding ceremony only once before, one of my mother's cousins. It'd been a small affair, just close family, and a few friends. But from what I'd overheard between Mom and Evelyn during their planning, all the Family Heads would be attending our ceremony, as well as nearly the entire Manser Family.

I watched the road signs as my mind spun, mentally following the map of Interstate 85, as it headed southwest to where we'd have to switch to I-20 in Alabama. Anything to try and not think about the nervous fluttering growing in my stomach. So when Dad took the exit off of 85 in Atlanta for I-75 South, I noticed.

"Wait, you're in the wrong lane." I watched helplessly as we merged into I-75 traffic. Then glanced back at him. "Why are we going this way?"

"There's something I want to show you first."

I crossed my arms against my chest, watching the minutes tick by on the dashboard clock, waiting for him to tell me more as we continued to drive further south and further away from Texas. After another hour of silence, I couldn't take it anymore. "Where are you taking me?"

"Just be patient; I promise we'll still make it to Texas in

time." Dad stayed mostly silent the rest of the way, only complaining about the traffic and the lack of good music on the radio. I kept my responses short if I said anything at all. This was ridiculous. Why couldn't he just tell me where we were going? It wasn't like I was a child, where the excitement of adventure was all that would keep me happy.

It was another two hours before he turned off the interstate and drove along the winding back roads. I must have fallen asleep at some point in the afternoon. Because when I woke up, Dad was pulling up to a pump at a small gas station. The sun was low on the horizon, the sky afire with orange and reds of the sunset as it shone through the ancient Spanish moss-filled trees that lined the roadsides.

Dad opened his door, and I sat up with a groan.

"Where are we?" I asked, hoping he'd give in and tell me.

"Almost there. Want anything from inside?"

Nodding, I untangled myself from the seat belt. I reached for Poe, letting him out to stretch his wings while Dad and I were inside.

I poured myself a coffee while waiting for Dad to come out of the restroom and grabbed a candy bar from the snack aisle.

"Three fifty," the old man behind the counter said. He looked up at me and swore, putting a hand to his heart.

"Mother Mary, you're one of them Reinhardt's, ain't you, boy?"

My body froze. Was he a witch? Why was he asking? My brain was running too fast to think.

"Uh, what?"

He nodded to me, pointing at my chest. "That there necklace, where'd you get it?"

I looked down to see the pendant on the outside of my shirt. I usually wore it hidden underneath, but it must have fallen free while I slept in the car. "Oh, it was, um, given to me by a friend." I passed over my cash quickly. "Why do you ask?"

Dad came up next to me with his own coffee and snack, and a worried look in his eye.

"Hmph, you got that look about you. Looked like you might be one of their kids that were always running in here. They were always wearin' charms and the like, like that." He paused, passing me my change. "That was years ago they stopped coming in here. That ain't right then, you're too young to be one of them kids."

I moved aside so Dad could pay for his stuff and the gas. "These Reinhardts, they live around here?" I asked.

"Yeah, or they used to, anyhow. I remember driving up by their place once after the kids stopped coming, just to check 'n' see if everything was alright. It was all boarded up. Not a soul in sight. Just gone."

Dad placed a bill on the counter. "Keep the change."

I followed him out the door, glancing back at the old man.

"We're going to the Reinhardt property?" I asked as he pulled open his door.

Poe cawed from where he sat on the roof rack and flew the few feet to perch on my shoulder.

"I thought you might want to see where the other summoners once were." His words were slow, painful almost. "Maybe we can find some of their reference books to help you with your Talent."

We were going to see the Reinhardt house, to see where my father had grown up and probably went through so many of the same problems and decisions I had as a Talentless. It made my chest tighten as I thought about it. "Yeah, that'd be great."

We got back into the car, and Dad pulled onto the country road. Holding my coffee, I watched the trees pass on the edge of the car's high beams. Even after everything I'd said the last few weeks, he still thought of doing something like this for me. He'd been distant ever since my test, but I also hadn't made a great effort to connect with him either. Maybe having to face the reality that I wasn't really his son had done something to him. Hurt him in some way, similar that it'd hurt me to learn that they weren't my 'real' parents.

I examined Dad out of the corner of my eye. He looked tired, and not just from the long day of driving, but the kind of weariness that comes after a long week or a bad few months. Mom and Dad, they had done what was best for me. They'd even let me go off to college when they were afraid of me running into Witches. Dad was right. They had treated me just like their own.

"Poe told me something a few weeks ago when I started walking up to the Vault," I started quietly. "I had asked him about how I'd gotten to the Vault, the night you found me."

Dad glanced over at me before looking back at the road. "What did he say?"

I picked at the rim of my Styrofoam cup. "He told me who my biological parents were, kind of."

"Were?"

"The Witches caught up with them, made it look like an accident. My birth father was Talentless, but his parents were Reinhardt and Stanwood. I think that's why Poe chose to bring me to you and mom because we have the same blood."

I watched Dad's eyes soften a little, and after a few long minutes, he said, "I'm sure they would be proud if they were to see you now."

Settling back into the seat, I watched the stars wink through the passing trees, wondering just what it might have been like if my birth parents hadn't died.

We made it to the Reinhardt property just as true darkness fell. The moon had risen above the trees as Dad drove up the long gravel drive to the white plantation-style house that stood lonely in an empty field, the nearest trees thousands of feet away. He parked the car.

"Here we are, the Reinhardt Plantation."

The house looked a little run down, but nothing some work couldn't fix. The large, floor-to-ceiling windows of the first floor were boarded up, along with the front door.

I climbed out of the car and headed to the porch. The wooden boards creaked under my weight. Poe flew to my shoulder, giving a quiet caw as Dad approached with a flashlight to help me remove the boards before unlocking the doors.

We stepped into the dusty foyer, surveying the grand staircase to the second floor that dominated the entryway. "Do the other Families know about this place?" I asked.

"I'm sure the other Heads and possibly a few of the older generation." He searched to the left of the door, and the chandelier over the staircase came to life, bathing the room in light. "We weren't as serious back then about keeping the locations of our homes secret. It was only after what happened here to the Reinhardts that we all decided to move and keep our homes hidden."

"And you just happened to have the keys?" I glanced back at him before moving into an adjoining room. The furniture was draped in large sheets of dusty cloth.

Dad followed me, tucking the keys into his pocket. "The Reinhardts and the Stanwoods always had a close relationship. Our two families often mixed, one of the last marriages before the war rumped up was between my aunt and uncle. I came back with my Mom and uncle after Aunt Emily was killed, to help pack the house. Since she was one of the last..."

His voice trailed off as he turned to inspect the fireplace mantel, and I kept moving through the room, not wanting to push. Poe launched from my shoulder, flying back to the foyer to land on the banister.

"How does this place still have power?" I asked as the thought occurred to me.

"I made some calls last week. Got the utilities working again." He walked over to stand next to me. "I thought you'd at least want to see the place. Maybe, after we fix it up a bit, you and Avery could live here. If you want to, that is. Come on, the office was on the second floor, if I remember right," Dad said, starting for the stairs.

Following automatically, I was stunned. Dad was right, I thought watching Poe flew ahead of us. I was a Reinhardt now, where else should I be?

We walked along an empty hallway with doors that stood open to rooms filled with more draped furniture. Faint outlines of picture frames and nails littered the yellowed papered walls. Dad stepped into a doorway at the end of the hall.

"This is it," he said, ducking a little as Poe glided in after him to perch on the back of a draped armchair.

There were dark, wooden, floor-to-ceiling bookshelves built into the walls that reminded me of Dad's study back home. The only difference was these shelves were dusty and bare of books. Instead, file boxes were piled high, hiding the bottom shelves. I pulled the top off the closest one to me and found it full of the missing books.

Glancing around the room, I counted the boxes. There were well over a dozen. "We can't take all of these, there's not enough room in the car."

"I wasn't planning on it," Dad said, lifting a box onto the cloth-covered desk. "I thought we could go through them tonight and see if any would be helpful to you right away. We can come back for the rest later." He started sifting through the books.

I turned back to my box, shuffling the volumes. Some were leather-bound, and some were so old that the bindings looked like they'd been sewn by hand. Many books were written in languages I didn't recognize.

Poe watched me with a curious look, tilting his head in the way birds do.

"I don't suppose you could tell me which ones I need?" I asked him, knowing better than to expect any sort of answer.

He gave a caw, and a loud, hollow click sounded over by the desk. Dad and I stared at each other for a moment, then I straightened and walked over to where I'd heard the sound. As I rounded the corner of the desk, I could see one of the wooden floorboards had popped out of place.

"Did he just..." Dad's words trailed off in disbelief.

I shrugged before kneeling to pry the board free, finding a hidden compartment underneath, and in that, a safe. I tried to move more of the thin wooden boards and found that the few right above the safe's door came free easily. The safe itself wasn't big, it looked about the size that could be found in hotel closets to store valuables.

Poe glided down to the floor, stepping carefully in that awkward bird step until he stood on the other side of the enclosure. He pecked at the combination lock.

"That's interesting. I never knew the Reinhardt's had that," Dad said, leaving the box on the desk to come inspect the safe. "I've got a few tools in the car-"

I held a finger to my lips, interrupting him. Poe was still pecking at the safe, which I'd thought was odd at first until I heard the rhythm. After turning the dial in the combination Poe'd tapped, I reached for the handle. Power arched between my fingertips and the safe, like a little red burst of static. The small door popped open as a chill swept over my skin. It'd taken enough Talent from me that I was left wishing I'd brought my jacket in from the car.

Dad raised his eyebrows at me. "Impressive."

"I didn't do anything," I said, dismissively, looking to see what was inside. There were several heavy, leather-bound books and a velvet, drawstring pouch. I pulled the bag out, undoing the strings to open the velvet bag into my hand. Pendants, almost identical to my own, spilled out. There were fifteen in all, though smaller than mine, and the stones were black instead of red.

"I heard that the Witches would take the Reinhardt pendants as trophies. The other Necromancers could never find them when we collected the bodies." Dad picked one up, looking at it carefully before returning it to my hand. "These must have been for the children, the ones who hadn't awakened their Talent yet."

Not the whole line. Poe's words from before echoed in my mind. My head snapped up to look at the bird.

"I'm not the only Reinhardt that survived, am I?" I asked Poe. He eyed me with a steady gaze, as still as if he'd been stuffed.

I turned Dad. "There must be others! If I was able to escape from the Witches, there had to be others. Maybe some who were hidden like me."

Dad looked thoughtful. "If that's true, and it could be possible, we'd need to find them and soon. It'll be safer for them if they're with the Families."

He was probably right. And the thought of helping others out there finally learn the truth about who they really were, appealed to me.

Carefully, I put the pendants back in the bag and tied it shut, before turning my attention to the books. I pulled the oldest looking one out first; the tattered cover looked like it had been repaired and mended multiple times over the years.

On the inside cover, I found a detailed family tree that started with Francis Reinhardt at the top and spread down the page listing names, dates of births, and deaths. Children and marriages. After those pages came journal entries from Francis, all written by hand in a flowing script.

Setting the book aside, I pulled the next one out and found something similar, except in different handwriting. Another Head of the Family.

"These are journals," I said, looking up at Dad. "From the Heads of the Reinhardt."

Poe tapped at the last one stacked in the safe, shuffling his feathers a little. I pulled it out and found that it was the journal of Alan Reinhardt, the last Head before the fall of the Reinhardts to the Witches. While I was interested in the journal entries, what held my fascination was the family tree in the front.

Under Alan's name, were those of his three children: Connar, Ashton, and Emily. Emily Reinhardt had married Matthew Stanwood, and they had three children; the third of which, Adam, had been Talentless.

"Ezra?" Dad's concerned voice broke through the emotions that welled inside me. My face felt wet; I hadn't even realized I'd started crying. I wiped at my face impatiently.

"Adam and Samantha," I said, looking up at him as I handed the book over. "My birth parent's names were Adam and Samantha Stanwood."

Chapter 5

I shifted in my seat again, trying to get comfortable as I took the ramp off the interstate into the city the Mansers called home. We'd stayed the night at the Reinhardt house and driven straight through from Georgia. Dad and I took turns at the wheel, so we only had to stop to get gas and change drivers.

"We're supposed to be there already. Do you think they'd go ahead without us?" I asked, adjusting my grip on the steering wheel.

Dad rolled his head towards me, and I could only imagine the ridiculous look I got. "Ezra, it'd be a little hard to do the ceremony without Avery's bonded. I'm sure they won't start without us," he said dryly.

"Right." I rechecked the map, there was still a ways to go before we reached the Manser's ranch. "Ah, grab my cell phone out of my bag. You can call them."

"Ezra-"

"Please?"

Dad sighed, reaching into the backseat to pull my bag free of the boxes of books we'd piled in the backseat. Poe let out a squawk of protest, and I caught a flash of wings in the rearview mirror.

"This thing?" Dad asked.

I glanced over. He held my phone up. "Yes, Dad. That's a cell phone."

He grinned at me and pressed the power button. "I'm only kidding."

The phone played its start-up music and starting buzzing repeatedly with messages.

"When was the last time you checked this thing?"

I shrugged. "It's been a while. About when I left school, I guess."

"Who's John?" Dad asked.

"Hey- don't read them." I snatched the phone from him and tossed it in the map pocket. "He was my roommate. Forget it."

Dad was silent a few minutes while I concentrated on the road. Of course, John would have left messages. I hadn't been off the mountain at all since I'd returned home. Well, except for my test, but I doubt there was any sort of reception in the Half-World. So much had happened, I'd forgotten about school completely. I was so focused on my Talent, now that I'd finally had it. I glanced down at my phone, feeling a little guilty about not contacting John. He must think I'm a complete psycho.

"It's alright to have friends outside of the Families. You know that, right?" Dad said.

"Dad-"

"I wonder if your mother and I did the right thing, keeping you and Liam up on that mountain. I know it was safer, but you haven't had much of life or real friends."

I pulled the car up to a stoplight and looked over at him. "You did what you thought was best. The other families do the same. There's no telling what the Witches are doing now. I mean, when was the last time a Necromancer was attacked?"

He looked at me solemnly. "Last month, out in Portland. One of the Emerson's cousins was killed. He barely had enough power to hear the dead, and they still attacked him. Made it look like a house fire."

I stared at him. "I thought they'd stopped -'

A horn blared behind us. I looked back to the road and drove through the green-lit intersection before the diesel truck behind us decided it was in a monster rally.

"I thought the Witches had stopped killing after they couldn't find the rest of us Stanwoods?"

Dad stared out at the passing scenery. "No, the Heads decided to stop telling everyone about the deaths."

"What? Why?! That doesn't make any sense-" But as soon as the words left my mouth, I understood. "To keep the others from seeking revenge on the Witches? Is that why you didn't tell us?"

"There's more to it than that. We don't have the manpower we used to. The Reinhardts were our soldiers, and we also did our fair share of the fighting. The Witches took notice of that and aimed their attacks accordingly. If we tried to plan an all-out attack on them now, there's no way we can win."

My thoughts shifted to those who'd died at the hands of the witches. "But what about their families? What kind of justice do we offer them..." I let my words trail off. He couldn't tell them. That'd be where it would all start. Their loved ones would demand revenge, and we didn't have the power to seek it. All it would accomplish would be to kill us off faster.

"There's gotta be something we can do!"

"Maybe, eventually, but right now, all we can do is lay low and keep ourselves safe. Keep the children safe."

———

We pulled onto the Manser ranch about noon. It was set in the outskirts of Austin, forty sprawling acres of mostly pasture for the horses they boarded. While the Stanwoods lived off the herbs and exotic plants we grew in the greenhouses and sold through mail-order, the Mansers made their living through horses.

I parked next to all the other vehicles littering the grassy area in front of the large ranch house. The front door opened as soon as we pulled into the driveway, and Thea raced out to greet us, Mom and Avery not far behind.

Opening the back door, I reached in for Poe, allowing him to climb onto my arm. He stretched his wings out for balance as I moved him free of the car, turning to find Thea right beside me.

"May I?" she asked, but it was directed not me, but Poe himself.

He winged gently over to the girl's shoulder and she walked off without another word. The whole interaction gave me a chill.

"There you two are!" Mom said. "What took so long? I was out of my mind when Liam and I got here before you!"

Dad swept her into a hug. "We just took a little detour. We're fine."

She eyed him in a way that made me think he was going to get an earful about it later.

"Where have you been?" Avery rushed up to me, wrapping her arms around in me in a tight hug. "Everyone's here already! Even Nathan."

I frowned. "Wow, I didn't think he'd show up on time."

Dad opened the trunk and grabbed his bag. "He may be an ass, but he takes his duty as Head of the Ackland Family seriously."

"William!" Mom shrieked at him, and Dad only shrugged.

"What?"

She shooked her head as Avery and I smirked, too.

"Where'd you get all those books?" Avery asked, breaking the tension.

"I'll tell you about it later," I said and pulled my own bag free. I followed Avery up to the house, and for all the cars parked out front, the estate was quiet. The Manser family had been busy since their return, decorating the home from top to bottom. There were fresh-cut flowers everywhere. Light pink roses and violet-blue wildflowers lined the railing to the second story, sat in vases in the living room, and a large centerpiece sat on the dining room table. Broad sweeps of white fabric and satin bows were pinned up to the banisters and walls as well.

A pit settled in the bottom of my stomach. This was really happening.

"Do you like it?" Avery asked, bouncing at my side in excitement as she showed me into the room off the side of the living room that I'd be sharing with Liam.

I set my bag down and forced a smile to my face. "It's perfect."

She studied my face. "You don't like it," Avery said with a frown and sat on the couch.

"No, I do!" I said quickly, stepping over to her. "I just can't believe this is happening, you know?" I pulled her back to her feet, wrapping my arms around her. "I love it, promise."

She smiled and stretched up on her toes to kiss me. Her lips were soft and made me feel so light-headed, I thought I might float away.

A polite cough separated us faster than oil in water. I turned to see Nathan standing in the doorway in a grey suit and a hard expression.

"Ezra, if I may have a word."

I glanced at Avery, who shrugged, a blush lingering on her cheeks.

"I've got to go check on some preparations anyway. Dinner will be at five just so you know." Avery slid past Nathan as he stepped into the room.

Turning back to my bag, I picked it up to place on the couch. I unzipped it, waiting for Nathan to say something. Knowing him, it would probably be something nasty, or demeaning-

"I want to apologize."

My hands stilled as I turned to gawk at him. "What?"

"I said, 'I want to apologize.' I know that my treatment of you since we first met has been," he paused, searching for the right word. "...less than friendly."

Well, look at that. I didn't think it was possible. But still, it didn't feel right. I straightened. "What's this about?"

Nathan looked away from me, walking over to the window to glance out at the preparations in the backyard. "Did you know that my uncle was Talentless?"

I took a seat on the couch next to my bag. "No."

"He was the youngest of four. You know how Talent tends to run out with a family so large, there just simply wasn't any left for him." Nathan turned back to me. "It drove him mad. The constant studying, straining to reach something that would never be his. He eventually took his own life."

Nathan was opening up to me, and I couldn't believe what my ears were hearing. "I'm sorry," I said, trying to think of something more.

He shook his head. "I just didn't want the same to happen to you. I wanted to push you to go and find a passion that would take you away from the Families, that would give you a purpose your missing Talent couldn't give you." He glanced at me. "I didn't want to see such a young life wasted in endless pursuit."

"So, you were mean to me?"

He shrugged. "Tough love. You didn't need another father in your life."

Nathan had no idea how true that statement was.

"I reacted badly the last time the Families met. To imagine, that the Reinhardt powers had been reborn in you, that we haven't lost so great a Talent..." he shook his head again. "I just couldn't fathom it.

"To show my sincerest regrets, I would like to offer you a gift." He snapped his fingers, and Collen appeared in the doorway so quickly that he must have been waiting in the hallway. He hurried over to his father with a large velvet box in his hands. I stood as Collen opened it, displaying a selection of rings. Engagement rings.

"To show that I, nor any of the Acklands, have a grudge against you or your bonded. I confess I didn't know which kind you would like, so I brought a selection for you to choose from. They're all Avery's size, of course, so don't worry about that."

I stared at the box. There were easily over twenty rings to choose from. Hundreds of thousands of dollars worth of diamonds. "I can't accept this. Even just one of them, it's way too expensive!"

"Please, I insist. Think of it also as a wedding gift, if you will." He took the ring box into his own hands, holding it closer to me for inspection.

I hesitated, glancing over the selection to stall while I thought of another excuse not to chose one. But then my eyes fell on one. It was perfect. The ring was the most modest and simple of the bunch, but the style just screamed Avery at me. I reached for it before I could stop myself.

"Ah, the Willowlark, an excellent choice. It will definitely suit her style, I think." Nathan plucked it from the velvet and held it out to me.

"I really couldn't..." I started to protest again, but even I could tell my will was crumbling. I would never be able to afford something this nice on my own.

Nathan smiled in victory and placed the ring in a smaller ring box before pressing the set into my hand. "Avery deserves the very best."

Turning the box over in my hand, I glanced up at him. The years of hatred and grief he'd given me couldn't just be washed away over one conversation. But this was a new start for both of us. As it was, we would eventually be equals in rank.

"Thank you," I said slowly as Nathan turned for the door.

"Congratulations," Collen said and followed his father out of the room, just as Liam came in.

"Hey, Ezra, they need you in the living room. Something about fittings."

I stuffed the ring box in my bag, not wanting to show anyone else just yet. "Alright, I'll be there in a minute." I hadn't had a moment to myself yet and was starting to feel a little too warm. My power was building again, and I would need to find time to do some of the exercises Poe had given me to bleed some of it off.

I escaped into the backyard after being tortured by my mother and her dressing pins for an hour. Poe's screech caught my attention, and I found him sitting on an open stall door of the stable. He took off, gliding away from me toward the grove of trees that sat in the middle of the Manser's land. I followed, walking through the pastures dotted with horses, looking forward to a chance to release some power and meditate.

The hemlock trees encircled a small clearing where a stone altar was set up. Potted plants and flowers were placed around the wooden pillars that supported the massive, stone slab. I'd read once in one of old Stanwood books that the Manser's altar was the oldest relic in all of the Necromantic Families. It'd had been moved only once when the Mansers fled the Witches from their previous estate in Montana.

Taking a seat in the grassy clearing facing the altar, I criss-crossed my legs in front of me and took a deep breath. Talent crawled along my arms, like thousands of tiny spiders. Shoving my worries about tomorrow's ceremony aside, I cleared my mind of all the questions I had about the Reinhardts and my lingering doubts about Nathan's intentions. I focused instead on my power. Controlling it, pulling all the warmth that radiated from my skin back into myself, and shaping it into a ball of energy at my core.

But as soon as I got the ball to form, I'd feel the energy slip away as my concentration wavered, and I had to start the process all over. It was aggravating.

The Talent raced along my skin and the more I attempted to control it, the faster it slipped from my fingers. I let everything go and cleared my mind again. There was a stillness that hung around the altar, that even the breeze couldn't touch as it whispered through the trees. The new spring leaves sang against each other as the birds added their own chorus to the nature song.

I reached for my Talent and this time, it came willingly, gathering itself tightly into the ball and stayed there. Having it all in one place was taxing and a little frightening. The sheer amount was more than I thought I could ever have. It was too much to release in a spark like that night in my bedroom. It would be more like a lightning bolt, with me at the end of it.

Decision made, I opened my eyes. "*Vershala tulian das lo berruas.*"

The red circle glowed bright and violent against the grass in front of me. "*Kalha vas notha rak! Kastem!*" I released the Talent into the spell, enjoying the rush of cooling sensation racing along my skin as the summoning circle shrank to a pinpoint, then exploded in a burst of light. The doglike demon, Kastem, stared at me, waiting.

I sent the demon a silent command, but Kastem ignored me. Instead, he chose a spot in the clearing as far as possible from me and lay out in the sun. To say that the connection between us was strained would be an understatement. But, maybe that could change in time.

The snap of a twig set both Kastem and I both on edge. I turned to see Avery standing near one of the trees.

"Sorry, I didn't mean to scare you."

I shook my head. "You're fine," I said, and silently told Kastem she was not to be harmed, that she was a friend.

The demon stood and walked up to her, his multiple tails high like a banner. I stood and followed, trying not to let my worry show.

Avery offered a hand to the beast. "He seems so much friendlier than the last time I saw him."

Shrugging, I watched the two of them interact, ready to dismiss the demon back to the Half-world at the first sign of aggression. "He really isn't all that bad, I guess."

The silence stretched between us as Avery affectionately patted and scratched the demon's head like he was a giant pet dog. He stood tall enough that his head came up to her chest.

Avery's hand stilled on top of Kastem's head. "I found something today." Her voice was slow, its expression unsure. "I've been going through my Dad's office, getting it organized for when it's all official." She reached into the back pocket of her jeans and pulled out an envelope.

Avery opened it and handed me a bit of folded paper. "We've some extended family out near Virginia Beach. They wrote about some - disturbing news. They claim the Witches have started gathering forces and supplies again."

"What?" I said, dismissing Kastem with a thought as I unfolded the paper.

There was urgency in her voice. "It was overnighted the day before Dad died, so it's been on his desk this whole time..."

I stared at her for a breath of a moment before skimming the letter. It detailed a few dates from the days before Mr. Manser's death. The location was a cluster of warehouses along the coast of Virginia. Listed below were items that didn't seem to make any sense. Different types of wood, essential oils and herbs, and a large number of unspecified planets.

"How much of this can we trust?" I asked Avery slowly, looking at her over the edge of the letter.

She shrugged. "The Hendersons are known for their accuracy, and they take extra care when it comes to Family business. Dad used to say they were his favorite spies." She paused, reaching for the letter. "Although, I will admit they are still upset about the war with the Witches. It was a concern of mine as I started helping Dad with some stuff last year."

"You don't think they would plant the evidence, do you? Make it seem like the Witches are up to something to force our side to attack?"

"I hadn't thought about that." She frowned at me a moment. "No, I don't think they would."

I glanced at the letter again. "What are you going to do?"

She shook her head. "I want to be sure before I have to tell the other Heads. I don't want to say something and have it turn out to be a mistake."

"We could always go and check it out ourselves-"

"Wait, now?" Avery's eyes widened. "We can't leave now! Not only is it crazy dangerous, but we're also about to do the ceremonies. We can't just go wandering off into Witches circles."

"We'll leave tomorrow night after the ceremonies. If we can find some concrete evidence, then we can tell the others."

"Tell the others what?"

I turned and found Liam standing behind us. He looked at each of us in turn, a worried expression forming on his face.

"What's going on?" he asked, the scars on his left cheek pulling a little as he frowned.

Glancing at Avery, I waited for her. The letter was intelligence from her family. It wasn't my place to share the news. That had to be her decision.

She studied the piece of paper in her hand a moment longer before stepping across the clearing to pass it to Liam.

He looked confused at first, but his eyes grew wider as he skimmed the letter. "Is this true?" he asked, looking sharply at her.

Avery shrugged. "We were just discussing it. Ezra and I want to be absolutely sure before we tell the other Families." She paused, looking at her hands. "This could bring about an all-out war. People's lives, our lives are at stake. I have to know for sure, I want to authenticate it before I say anything to the Heads."

Liam's eyes returned to the paper, reading it one more time. He passed it back to her when he finished. "How are you going to verify the information?"

I took a deep breath, preparing for the argument I knew was coming. But Avery beat me to it. "We're going to go see for ourselves," she said. "We'll leave tomorrow night."

He looked at us as if I'd just walked over and slugged him across the face.

"Are you insane?!" he yelled. "You just can't go wandering off looking for Witches! That's how you get yourself killed. Besides, how are you even going to get there?"

Liam's question hit me as hard.

"We'll take my car," I said, slowly calculating everything we would need. Money for food and gas was a priority. How would we manage that without involving our parents?

Liam's gaze narrowed at us. "I thought so. You haven't thought this through it all."

"That doesn't mean anything," I argued. "Avery just found this. Of course, we need a few hours to plan a trip out."

He scoffed. "Just a few hours?"

"Enough!"

Poe's voice erupted from the trees behind us. I turned in time to see him step up to the altar in his human form.

"Your bickering is giving even the birds headaches."

Liam and Avery step back, worry on their faces.

"How?" I asked. "I thought you said only in the Vault –"

Poe shrugged, waving a hand at the air around him. "This place is sacred ground, like Stanwood Vault. I can stay this way within the grove."

"Do you know this man?" Liam asked, coming to stand beside me. The cool brush of his power brought goosebumps to my skin.

"It's Poe."

Liam shot me a look of disbelief as Poe turned his attention to Avery and held out a hand.

"May I see the letter?"

Avery glanced at me. I nodded, and she handed over the letter. Poe read through it quickly before handing it back to Avery.

"What do *you* want to do?" he asked her.

She glanced at Liam and me. "We were just discussing that."

Poe hoisted himself up to sit on the altar. "But ultimately, it is your decision as Head of the Manser family."

Avery gave him a startled look. "But Ez and-"

"They can offer suggestions and opinions, but the decision is yours alone, just as it will be for them when they become the heads of their own Families."

"What about your opinion? What do you think I should do?" Avery asked.

Poe glanced around at us and sighed. I don't think I'd seen him look so exhausted before. "I think they are both right."

"How can we both be right?" I asked.

"Liam is right because it is a fool's errand to go out there unprepared and alone. However, I also agree with you. You are right to question such a letter. Confirming its validity is a good idea."

I turned back to Avery, trying to think of something else that might help her. She stared at the letter in her hand.

"We have to find out if what my cousins wrote is true, and I'd rather wait to involve the other Heads of the families until I know for sure. I would hate to stir up unnecessary trouble."

"This is insane!" Liam shouted. "You're going to get yourselves killed."

Poe shot him a look that stopped his shouting as quickly as it started.

"I'm sorry you disagree," Avery said, folding her arms across her chest, "But I don't think there another choice."

I nodded. "We just need to figure out how to be smart about it and get it done quickly."

Liam threw his hands in the air. "I just can't with you all."

"If you're so concerned, come with us," Avery said. "You have more experience as a practitioner; you can be a big help."

He glanced at her, and for a moment, I thought he'd start yelling again. Finally, he closed his eyes and sighed. "Fine."

My eyes drifted toward the sky as the tension released in my body. "Now we just need to sort out the details. We'll have to drive, so when-"

"Actually," Poe interrupted, jumping down from the altar to step closer, "you don't. The key to this sort of mission is stealth and quickness. The faster you can get in and out, the better. For numerous reasons."

"How do we get there, then?" Liam quipped. "We don't exactly have the spare cash to take a flight."

Poe was quiet a moment as he studied us. "There is another way. A way that necromancers used to travel with the help of the Reinhardts."

Liam's eyes widened. "You can't be serious." He shifted the stare to me, looking more awestruck than upset.

"What?" I asked him.

Liam turned back to Poe. "Can Ezra really do that? Create portals like the Reinhardts could?"

I was so confused. What portals? I watched Poe's expression shift to careful thought.

"It can take years of training to manipulate portals. While Ezra cannot do that sort of spell at the moment, I have no doubt he will be able in the future."

"If not Ezra, then who?" Avery asked. "Who could open a portal for us to use?"

Poe gave a smug smirk. "I will open the portal. All you have to do is follow. It will not be difficult."

Liam gave him a look of respect. "If that's the case, then we might actually be able to pull this off. All we need to decide is when to leave, right?"

Avery nodded. "Tomorrow night, after the ceremonies. There's too much attention on Ezra and me at the moment, but no one would think twice of us disappearing for a few hours afterward." She blushed a deep crimson, avoiding my gaze.

I cleared my throat nervously. I really didn't need to think about putting the 'Birds and the Bees' talk into practice right this moment. "So tomorrow evening, then?"

Liam nodded. "We make it quick, less than an hour. In. Out. Back here ASAP."

"We meet here in the grove, then. Tomorrow after dark."

Poe jumped and shifted, taking on his other form to fly back towards the house.

"I had no idea," Liam mumbled, watching him. "What is he?"

I wish I knew how to answer that.

My alarm went off early the next morning, but it didn't matter. I was already awake. It felt like Christmas morning, but on top of being super excited, I was also insanely nervous.

Liam wasn't as thrilled with the wake-up call, but he stirred, crawling out of his makeshift bed to pull a shirt on and escape out the door. I rolled myself deeper into the blanket, taking a few extra moments to myself in the comfort of warmth. Avery's mother kept the house *cold*. And even with my powers to keep me warm, I didn't want to leave my bed.

A knock on the door drew me out of my circling thoughts of what I was about to do.

"Ezra." Dad's voice was soft, and when I didn't answer, he repeated himself louder.

"Yeah?"

"There's coffee and breakfast in the kitchen; it's time to get up and get ready."

I groaned and debated snuggling down further into the covers for another few moments. Instead, I threw the blankets off and grabbed a handful of clothes.

After I'd taken my turn in the shower, shaved, and dressed in my suit, I headed for the kitchen. Most of the men were gathered in the living room, looking tired and groggy.

Dad passed me a travel mug of coffee.

"Thanks," I said, and sipped at it.

"Let me give you a piece of advice that my father gave me

when I married your mother," he said, fiddling with the top of his own mug. "Never take her — or anything — for granted. Be grateful every day for the life you have and the love you've found."

A door opened upstairs, and I could see the moms and aunts pour out of Avery's room onto the landing.

Mom and a few of the others came down first. She came to stand near Dad and me, reaching out to adjust my tie. "Are you ready?"

I swallowed, nodding a little. "Yeah, I think so."

A hush fell over the crowd as everyone turned to see Avery standing at the top of the stairs. She descended slowly, carefully, and I couldn't help but stare at her.

In the flowy knee-length pink dress, with her hair curled and pulled back to tumble in spirals down her back, she was stunning.

At that moment, what really mattered became clear to me. Avery and I were about to promise ourselves to each other, and no matter what the world threw at us, we'd be facing it together. I could see in her eyes she wanted this just as much as I did, erasing my fears of coercion.

Someone took my coffee, and I soon found myself at the bottom of the stairs, holding an arm out for her. Her hand shook a little, so I covered it with one of my own.

The Families parted before us, lining a path to the back door and the waiting ceremony.

"Ready?" I whispered.

She nodded slightly and accepted a small bouquet of flowers from Thea, who stood at her elbow.

We stepped out into the chilly morning, the pre-dawn light just starting to brighten the sky as we crossed the damp grass to the flower-and-ribbon arch that had been put up at the tree line of the grove. Poe circled above us before swooping in and landing on my shoulder. After a gentle squeeze of his talons, he took off again to settle atop the arch.

Usually, it was the Head of the Bride-to-be's family that would lead the ceremony, but in this case, Avery had asked my father to step in. Dad met us at the arch as everyone gathered behind us.

As the sun broke over the eastern horizon, the ceremony began. Dad held a small, sheathed knife in his hands. He smiled as each of us in turn, then looked out to those who'd assembled behind us.

"We are gathered here this morning to witness and celebrate a vow of commitment between two people. Today they promise to dedicate themselves to learning about each other in joyous times and through struggle. In health and in sickness. We stand here, two families joined as one, happy not only to witness the beginning of a new journey for Avery and Ezra but because they have the opportunity to express their aspirations for the future."

Dad motion to Avery and me, and we turned to face each other. He drew the knife from its casing and held it out to me hilt first. I took it carefully and positioned the point at the base of my ring finger on my left hand. I took a deep breath.

"I, Ezra William Stanwood, take you, Avery, to be my bonded. To hold in friendship and love until the day we go our separate ways. I will trust and honor you. I will laugh and cry with you. Through the best and the worst of times, through the difficult and the easy. Whatever may come, I will be there beside you. I give you my hand to hold as we start this journey together."

I pressed the knife into my skin. I didn't feel anything at first as I watched the blood well up around the blade. A testament to how sharp it was.

Avery took the knife as I handed it over. She placed the blood-stained tip on her left hand in the same place I'd cut mine. Her eyes then focused on mine, capturing my heart with her blue gaze.

"I, Avery Christine Manser, take you, Ezra, to be my bonded. To hold you in friendship and love until the day we might go our separate ways. I will trust and honor you. I will laugh and cry with you. Through the best and the worst times, through the difficult and the easy. Whatever may come, I will be there. I give you my hand to hold, as we start this journey together."

She smiled nervously at me, and cut her hand, just as I had mine. After passing the knife back to my father, Avery reached for me, and we clasped our wounded hands together so that the blood and the cuts pressed against each other.

It was a rush of energy, a tingling zap that shocked its way through my system, leaving in its wake an undeniable pull to Avery. If either of us were ever lost, we would be able to find our way back to each other. All we'd have to do is follow our hearts.

The ritual part completed, I followed her gaze as she looked to my father.

He held a white satin ribbon up and started to tie it around our clasped hands.

"May you know nothing but happiness, may the road rise up to meet you, and may the wind be always at your back." He smiled at us both, finishing the knot in the ribbon. "May your time together be happy."

I turned back to Avery and leaned in to kiss her on the cheek. Cheers and applause sprang to life behind us. We moved as one to face our combined Family.

Chapter 6

Avery stepped away from me and followed the other Family Heads into the trees. Anticipation gathered in the crowd behind us, a collective hush over all the members of the Manser family.

Mom came up to stand next to me, gently taking the ribbon from my hands and folding it without undoing the knot.

"How long-" I started to ask, but talking at the moment felt wrong.

She shrugged. "With your father, it was only a few minutes, but from what he's told me, it could take all day. It seems to depend on the person." Mom kept her voice low, and she glanced at the others standing between us and the house. All the Mansers stood still, staring into the trees like they were in a trance.

"What's happening?" I'd never seen anything like it.

Liam answered, "It's a calling. It reaches out to all those with the Manser blood in their veins. The Heads of the Family do more than just lead us, they tie us together as a whole. Right now, Dad and the others are helping Avery establish a new connection with each and every Manser out in the world."

My eyes widened at that thought, but I thought of what would happen when it was my turn. From what I'd gathered between Poe and the books from the old house, I would be the next Reinhardt Family Head. But could I would go through the same ceremony of connecting myself to the remaining Reinhardts? Would I be able to find them all that way? Could I be the one to bring them back together after all this time? Would they even know how important they were to the Necromantic community?

My head spun with questions, and for a moment, I felt completely overwhelmed by the responsibility lying before me. Could I really be someone so important?

The trance broke over the Manser family. They moved, blinked, and stretched, and a few minutes later, Avery and the other Heads appeared, walking out from the trees.

A cheer swept up, and everyone rushed forward to greet their new leader. Mom and I and the others who weren't Mansers hung back, watching as the somber mood turned joyous and festive.

The party lasted all day. Grills, smokers, and fire pits were lit, music was danced to, and for the most part, everyone relaxed. As the sun sank lower in the sky late that afternoon, I slipped away to my room. I changed quickly into some dark washed jeans, a black t-shirt, and a hoodie. I grabbed my messenger bag and stuffed it with a change of clothes and my phone before heading out to my car parked out front. Dodging Avery's family and mine wasn't the easiest feat, but most of the party was still in the backyard.

I popped open the trunk and grabbed the first aid kit and the flashlight. Pausing, I focused on the books from the Reinhardt house. I hesitated, debating with myself. It was just a quick trip out and back, and I definitely wouldn't have a chance to read at all. But still, the idea of taking one along plagued me. I opened a few, skimming quickly through the pages and settled on one that looked like it was full of incantations. I shoved it in my bag, immediately more comfortable knowing I had it with me.

But something was still missing. I couldn't think of what else might be handy to have, though. It wasn't like I did this sort of thing all the time.

I walked the long way around the house instead of heading back inside. I was in the clear now and didn't want to get sucked in a conversation about my plans for the future by one of Avery's well-meaning aunts.

Dusk had fallen, and only a slight glow sat on the horizon as a cold, spring breeze picked up enough to rustle the leaves. I came through the trees to the clearing and tossed my bag to the ground. Liam was already there, standing near the altar with his own backpack slung across his shoulders.

"I still think this is a bad idea," he said solemnly.

I didn't answer. When Liam got into a mood, it was best just to leave him alone. At least he was still coming with us and hadn't ratted Avery and me out to our parents.

Poe drifted down from the trees, landing lightly on my shoulder. There was just enough light from the half-full moon to see Liam's expression become cautious.

Steps sounded behind us, and I turned to see Avery come into the clearing.

She looked nervous and shaken. "Everyone ready?"

"Are you?" Liam replied.

Poe left my shoulder to shift forms and stand in front of us. The wind caught his dark coat and lank hair, almost as if in a weak attempt to rip them from him.

"We stay together," he said, looking at each of us in turn. "Once we're through, I won't be able to talk to you. See what you can, and when you're ready, I'll create another portal to bring you back. Don't take any unnecessary risks. Not for this."

Avery and I nodded as Poe turned his back on us and lifted his hands up, palms out.

I felt as he reached for his power, my own bubbling up in response. I had to focus on keeping it from overpowering my control.

The wind picked up as Poe started the incantation and whipped around him like a small dust devil, blowing twigs and debris outwards. When his voice rose an octave higher, a summoning circle appeared, but it wasn't like when I used my Talent. It grew out from a pinpoint, slowly, as if Poe's incantation had to coax it into existence. It was also vertical, parallel a few inches from Poe's outstretched palms.

The summoning circle spun slowly, then wildly as Poe's voice sped up. When it shrank in on itself, something very different happened afterward. Instead of exploding out in a burst of light, the point grew, agonizingly slow, into an oblong opening showing a moonlit beach.

"I can't hold this forever," Poe growled.

After a brief glance at Avery, I picked up my bag and shouldered it. Liam stepped up behind Poe and looked back at us.

"I'll go through, count to five, and follow." He didn't wait for a response, only turned and walked through the portal like it wasn't a huge deal.

Me? I was a little nervous. The last time I faced one of these, I'd fought for my life and barely made it out.

Trepidation must have shown on my face because the next thing I knew, Avery grabbed my hand and pulled me into the portal.

I stepped through the portal and on to the sand. The ocean's roar was deafening after the quiet evening in the grove. I moved away from the portal, crouching low in the underbrush of ferns and reeds that grew between the dead-end road and the surf.

Liam stood off a little way, looking disoriented. I grabbed his hand and pulled him down next to me. The last thing we needed was for someone to spot us before we even had a chance to get started.

The portal started closing, shrinking in on itself. At the last minute, Poe came flying through, circling in ever-larger arcs.

"Okay, I didn't think that was actually possible." Avery took a deep breath, still looking wild. "What now?"

"Now," I said, "we see what we can find. Can I see the letter again?"

She handed it to me as I dug out my phone and used the light from the screen to read the directions Avery's cousin listed in the letter. I glanced around in the darkness. The moon was already lower in the sky. We'd have to make this fast.

A large, fenced-in warehouse stood across the road. The metal siding tattooed in faded graffiti, and the windows were dark rows staring out at the sea. Poe had brought us almost exactly where we needed to be. I'd have to ask him how he'd managed that. I would have been too afraid of the Witches sensing the residual magic from the portal.

"What are we going to do now?" Liam asked.

I pointed at the warehouse. "We've got to get in there."

"Oh, well, that's easy. Let's just walk in the front door." He gave me a hard look. "There are probably cameras everywhere. How are we going to manage that without getting caught?"

"Very carefully," I said absently, thinking as quickly as I could. "Do you remember that time in middle school? We were in the barn while you were practicing one of the script spells? Do you remember how you kept getting it wrong?"

"I don't see how that's relevant to the moment, Ezra."

"Think about it," I insisted. "Why did Dad come out and make you stop?"

He paused for a moment, but then answered, "Because it was messing with the electricity in the house. I kept blowing out the fuses." Liam turned back to the warehouse. "I don't know if I could replicate that. I can't even remember what I did wrong."

I adjusted my bag, stopping it from cutting into my neck. "You didn't ground it right and created a feedback loop."

Liam shared a look with Avery before she asked, "How do you even remember that?"

"I was obsessed with Talent. You notice everything when you're obsessed." I glanced up, trying to find Poe against the inky black sky. "We should hurry before we're seen. Can you do it?"

"I can try." Liam's voice was uncharacteristically soft, and it didn't inspire the highest confidence. I clamped a hand on his shoulder.

"Let's get closer before you do anything."

We crept through the tall grasses, across the road and to the fence that lay just beyond. There was a gate where the fence met the road at the dead end, with a small, one-man guardhouse to go with it. Poe drifted down and perched on the roof. He let out a caw that was almost drowned in the sound from the surf.

As quietly as we could, we moved, keeping low. Liam was the first to reach the guardhouse. He peered over the window ledge.

"It's empty," he whispered.

I moved past him and tried the door. It was unlocked, but

the door itself stuck in the frame. I forced it as gently as I could, cringing at each noise it made as it came open.

Liam and I stepped inside. Avery stood at the door; there wasn't enough room for her.

"Try and get just the cameras?" I asked Liam.

"Right." He rubbed his hands together as if trying to warm them. Liam closed his eyes and took a breath.

Stanwood Talent differed from the Reinhardts. Everything I did had an incantation, words that had to be said to make anything work. Liam stood quietly, his focus inward.

I knew exactly what he was thinking, feeling almost. He would concentrate first on finding his cold power, pulling it to the surface slowly, carefully. Then, once the Talent was ready, he would shape it, warping it to work the spell.

Liam opened his eyes. They were frosted over with Talent, showing nothing of his pupils or irises. Wisps of cold fog rose from his outstretched hands.

"There," Liam said, his eyes clearing. "I've no idea if-"

"It worked," Avery said, her head popping in the door frame.

I stepped outside next to her. "How do you know?"

She pointed to the top corner of the closest building, where a camera was mounted under a security floodlight. It was smoking.

I glanced back at Liam. "Great work."

He sighed. "Let's just get this done."

We slipped through the gap in the fence where the chain and padlock left enough room for a person to slip through.

The place was deserted. I expected guards at least, maybe witches hanging around. Were the Henderson's wrong? Was this just an ordinary warehouse?

Questions rattled around my mind as unease grew in the pit of my stomach.

I kept close to Avery, her presence steadying mine as we ran across the open parking lot to the side of the closest building. Dirty windows lined the wall in the shadows; there wasn't a door on this side.

Using the sleeve of my hoodie, I tried to clean a spot on the window to see through, but it didn't help. They were as dirty on the inside as on the outside, but the window moved slightly. I worked my fingers under the lip and found it unlocked. Pulling it outward slowly, I ducked my head under it to peek inside. There wasn't anyone in sight.

"What are those?" Avery asked. She and Liam looked in from beside me, as Avery pointed out shadowed pallets of boxes that towered, creating a mini-city of cardboard surrounded by plastic wrap to keep them from toppling. Bundles of lumber were piled to the far side.

"Only one way to find out." I climbed in carefully, still hyper-aware of every tiny noise I made. After I was in, I turned and helped Avery over the sill as Liam held the window, then did the same as Liam worked his way in.

We walked through rows of pallets and wood, pausing to listen for any activity that wasn't our own. Avery also stopped every so often to check labels on the boxes, comparing it to the letter using a little flashlight she'd dug out of her bag.

"It's all the same," she whispered after catching up with me. "Everything is here, the different types of wood, the oils, and herbs. That's all of it, except the plants they mentioned."

I turned, surveying the space. "There is another building next to this one, maybe that's where the plants are."

Liam turned his own flashlight on us. "This isn't enough proof?"

We were running out of time, but the more information we could get now, the better prepared we'd be to tell the others. I bit my lip and looked at Avery.

"Let's take a quick look and see if we can figure out what kind of plants they are. Then we'll go."

Liam opened his mouth to argue more but was cut off by the sound of a door opening on the other side of the warehouse. It echoed through the darkness, freezing my heart. Avery and Liam switched off their lights as we rushed silently towards the open window. I glanced back once to see another beam swing through the darkness.

We reached the window and pushed it open slowly; now wasn't a good time to have it squeak.

Liam held the window open as I helped Avery through and then climbed out after her. I kept the window steady as Liam climbed through and closed it slowly again. We crouched low under the window, our backs against the corrugated metal siding.

My breath and pulse were racing, and I tried to steady my nerves. That had been close.

"We need to leave. Now." Liam's whisper came just inches away from my ear.

I shook my head. "We've got to see the other warehouse. Maybe grab one of those plants."

The window above us creaked, and I froze.

"Stupid windows," a voice said above us. "They really need to fix those." The window banged shut, muffling the voice.

Holding my breath until I could no longer hear him, I let it out in a slow stream while we waited in silence.

After what felt like years, Liam spoke softly. "We need to leave. I don't want us to get caught-"

"What, like we do?" I whispered harshly back at him.

"That's what it seems-"

"Enough," Avery said and stood. "Let's just get moving." She started towards the other warehouse, trying to look everywhere at once.

I followed after her, not waiting to see if Liam would follow. He'd agreed to come, he wouldn't abandon us.

The other warehouse was a story taller than the first. The

only entrance we could find was a staircase to a door on the second floor.

Climbing the stairs, I stayed close to the side of the building.

Poe flew in, landing on the railing. I tried the door once I reached it, and found it locked. Avery stepped up beside me and touched the door. I felt the barest whisper of her power as she closed her eyes.

"It's just a simple deadbolt," she said and frowned. A hollow thud sounded from the door as the bolt slid back. She looked up at me and smiled. "Sneaking in and out of the house as a kid had a few benefits."

She eased the door open and peeked inside. "It's clear."

I smiled at her as she held the door. Liam and I slipped past. I was looking for anything that might be out of the ordinary for a warehouse. What I found was pretty odd.

There wasn't a floor inside at the level of the door. Just a metal catwalk that circled around the perimeter and cut across the warehouse. I walked up to the railing, looking out over the scene before me. The actual floor was sunken, concrete slabs two stories below where we all stood. Rows of hydroponic bays filled the warehouse. The special UV grow lights, bright and artificial, ran on noisy generators that sat off to the side. Hooded, white-robed figures moved along the rows, tending to the plants. Witches.

"What in the world?" Avery whispered.

Liam made an impatient sound. "There are your 'plants.' Now can we go?"

I didn't even bother looking at him. "Not yet, we don't even know what kind of plants those are." I took a step out onto the nearest catwalk, but a hand jerked me back.

"Are you insane?!" Liam whispered. "What if someone sees us? What if they catch us? We are outnumbered, and there's no telling what they can do!"

Glancing back at Avery, I could see her resolve crumbling.

"We've seen enough," she said. "It's time to go back and tell the others." Avery moved back and bumped into the corner of the railing. The metal rattled against its fastenings, and the sound echoed through the warehouse. Loud enough to be heard over the generators. All the hooded figures below us turned, searching for its source.

"Up there!" One of them shouted, pointing at us.

Avery gave me a horrified look. We dashed for the door, but once we got there, it wouldn't budge.

"What the hell!" Liam said, jamming his shoulder against it.

"Guys!"

I turned to see what Avery was pointing at, and found the witches heading up the interior stairs to cut us off.

"This way," Liam shouted and grabbed Avery's arm. I followed them back onto the metal catwalk that led out over the plants. Witches were already on the other side, running towards us, but about halfway across the open space, a ladder rose to the roof.

Avery's voice was shaky when she asked, "What are we going to do?"

"We'll figure it out," I told her. "Just run!"

The catwalk rattled with each step. My heart raced, hoping the supports wouldn't give way with the next one. Liam reached the ladder first but pushed Avery in front of him.

"Quickly!" he urged as she climbed, and started up after her.

I watched the robed figures advance on either side, waiting until Liam got far enough up the ladder that I could climb on as well.

"Come on, climb faster!" I called.

Avery reached the skylight and pushed it open. She glanced back, looking past me with terror on her face.

Looking down, I saw the Witches right below, reaching for me. I kicked at their hands, but they grabbed hold. My grip on the ladder slipped, and I fell to the catwalk, my bag not doing much to cushion my landing.

"No-" Avery's scream was cut off as Liam tried to pull her away from the window. I knew he'd keep her safe.

"Just go! Find Poe," I yelled, fear gripping me as I watched more witches climb the ladder after them. Rough hands pulled at my arms, setting me upright.

Liam hesitated only a moment before disappearing from the skylight. One of the Witches caught my attention as they stepped in closer, reaching into their sleeve, revealing a small vial.

"Wait, what's that?"

"I'm sorry," he whispered as he closed the distance between us, and I could finally see into the shadows under his hood.

"J-" I started to say, but he took advantage of my surprise and forced the vial under my nose. The foul smell hit me instantly, making my body go limp. The last thing I saw before the blackness overtook me was the shape of a bird sitting on the edge of the skylight.

―――

I awoke to something sweet in the air, almost as if I'd been sleeping in a bakery. But that didn't make any sense. Why would I be sleeping there? I tried to move. My arms were pinned behind my back somehow, and whatever I was laying on was cold and hard.

"Set him up."

Hands grabbed at my arms, pulling me upright off the floor as the world spun around. I tried to catch myself before falling to the side, but I soon figured out that my arms were tied. A hooded figure caught me instead and held tight, so I wouldn't fall again.

My memory came back in a rush. The warehouses, the Witches. Avery and Liam escaping.

"What is your name, Necromancer?" The figure before me demanded in the same feminine voice from before. Her robe was different from the others that surrounded me. It was made of expensive cloth in a bright shade of green, with fine stitching of the same color scrolled along the edges. A Priestess, maybe?

"Your name," she commanded again, but this time pain shot up my arms.

I gasped, trying to think. I couldn't give the Witches my real name. "Asher," I breathed, thinking of a random name. "Asher West."

The green-hooded figure in front of me stepped closer, raising delicate hands to push the hood of her robe back to reveal dark, smooth skin, angled cheekbones and plush lips. She looked only a little older than I was. Her black hair was pulled up, to tumble in a waterfall of tiny braids around her shoulders. Her eyes narrowed, making me wonder if she knew I was lying.

"And how did you get in here, Asher West?"

I shrugged, and more pain lanced up my arms.

"Answer me," she demanded.

"The back door," I said the first thing that came to mind, which wasn't too far from the truth.

"And your friends. Where are they?"

"Anywhere, by now." And it was true. I could only faintly sense Avery, our connection pulled taut like an uncoiled spring. All I could say was that she was west of me, somewhere far west.

The witch clenched her jaw and glanced around the circle

of figures, all with their faces hidden deep within their white hoods. I was pretty sure she wanted to kill me on the spot.

"Why are you here?"

"No reason."

My head snapped to the side suddenly, my cheek stinging as if I'd been slapped. Except that she hadn't moved. No one had.

"I will not be so forgiving next time. I'll ask you once more, why are you here?"

I stared at her, not knowing what else to do. The hell I would tell her what we'd been doing. The last thing I wanted to do was send this back towards my Family, or the other Necromancers. It was all my fault. Liam had warned us, and I hadn't listened. I only hoped Poe had helped him and Avery back safely.

The Priestess tsked and snapped her fingers. The chains on my arms tightened and grew hot, the metal burning my skin.

"Let's see how you feel after a day in the bindings. Most men go mad."

She replaced her hood and turned on her heel to stalk away. Surprisingly, the others followed. I was left alone on the cold concrete floor, still trying to wrap my head around what had happened. I'd gotten caught. Then they'd knocked me out, but I forgot something.

The face in the hood, the guy with the vial who'd knocked me out. My memory blurred, and the more I reached for it, the faster the image slipped from me, like a dream the morning after.

They left my feet untied, but there wasn't anything in reach that would help free me. I twisted, gasping a little with the added pain, and tried to get a better look at what bound my arms together. All I managed to find was that the end of the chain they'd used was bolted to the floor. The more I struggled, the stronger the pain grew, making me light-headed and dizzy. Still, I fought it.

The warehouse around me was quiet. I was in a corner of the warehouse, on the other side from where Avery, Liam, and I had entered. The rows and rows of plants spread out in the center of the building still. At least they hadn't moved me far. If I could escape, if I could get out and away from the building, I might be able find Poe, or call Avery.

Light grew in the windows as day broke. Maybe I could do something with my power? Something to short-circuit the spell that caused the pain. I reached mentally for my Talent and screamed. The pain intensified, exploding a thousand times worse than before. Darkness stole over me again, and I ran towards it.

I fought to regain consciousness. The pain was the first thing I noticed. My arms felt like they were on fire, the chains tighter than before. The sun was brighter against the windows, the warehouse so silent I could hear the roar of the ocean faintly in the background. Was I still alone? How long had I been out?

The arm I was laying on started stinging with pins and needles as I shifted. It must have been awhile.

"You shouldn't have reached for your power. It's the worst thing you could do in a Binding." The voice came from behind me, but that wasn't what surprised me. What caught me off guard was that I recognized it.

Struggled to sit up, I turned to face the speaker. My roommate. John.

Now I remembered what was bothering me before - it was his face in the darkness of the hood as he knocked me out with the vial.

"How? Why are you here with the Witches?" I asked, still bewildered by John's presence. He sat cross-legged with the hood of his green trimmed white robe pushed back to show his face. Obviosuly, he was a Witch. How had I missed that before?

"What I want to know is how the hell *you're* a necromancer. When I last saw you three months ago, you didn't have any power. Necromancers are all the same: the rotting smell of death magic saturates their skin and only grows stronger. Tell me, *Asher*, how did you hide your power?"

The hurt in his words caught me by surprise.

"John, I..." I fought to find the words. "I didn't hide anything."

He rolled his eyes and got to his feet. "I thought we were friends. I thought you'd at least tell me the truth."

"It is!" He started to walk away, and desperately, I climbed unsteadily to my feet, following after him as far as the chain would allow. "John, I was Talentless. Do you know what that means in a family of Necromancers?"

He paused but didn't turn around.

"Sure, my parents loved me, but I was the black sheep, the outsider. For years I tried to find my power, and it never came. I went to college because I'd given up on being one."

John turned to face me, suspicion clear alongside the hurt in his eyes. "What happened? How come you're drenched in power now," he sneered at me. "Who'd you kill to gain it?"

His words twisted in my heart, hitting a little too close to home. I looked away as the girl's face filled my mind. I'd almost forgotten her. After all that had been going on between visiting the Reinhardt estate, the ceremonies, and Avery.

"It was my fault," I whispered, as raw pain filled me again.

The fact I'd stopped thinking about the girl who I'd failed to protect only made the guilt heavier.

"What?"

"I was supposed to protect her!" I screamed at him.

My power rose on its own, mirroring the rise in my emotions. It'd been too long since the last time I'd used it. Too much Talent had built up in me. I'd thought the burning from the Binding was terrible, but as the heat grew in my body now, it was like I'd stepped into a fire. I had no choice but to embraced it, to channel it before it burned me raw. "I was supposed to protect her, and I didn't."

John took a step back, confusion and fear playing on his face.

"Ezra, what-"

I couldn't stop the Talent. It felt like my arms were melting. The liquid fire spread upwards into my shoulders and down my back. The chains snapped, and I stood, facing John squarely. His eyes were wide, his skin pale.

"Ezra, what are you doing?!"

I froze. What was I doing?

Without even realizing, I'd closed the distance between us. My hand was outstretched, and I was focusing ...on something. On what?

"Let me go!" John's voice screamed.

Glancing down, I found that he was trapped. My summoning circle pulsing on the floor under him.

I dropped the power immediately, releasing him from the circle. I collapsed to the floor, exhausted. My hands were bright red with burns, my nails singed.

"Oh, Great ones, what did I do?" I whispered. After a moment's hesitation, I looked up, focusing on John. "Did I hurt you?"

He shook his head, still staring at me wide-eyed. "You're a summoner?" John's voice was breathless, terrified. "I thought...I thought they were all gone."

Looking around, the warehouse was silent. Deadly still. "Why aren't I being swarmed by Witches?"

John took a deep, shaking breath and ran a hand through

his hair. "I'm the only one here during the day. Everyone else has lives and jobs they can't miss."

"Even with a Necromancer here, they only left you?"

"They thought you were just a little no-name Necromancer. Why not leave you with an Apprentice?"

I stared at him. I couldn't believe I almost hurt him. Yes, he was a Witch, but he was also one of my few friends in this world. There wasn't an excuse for it. "John, I'm sorry. I am so sorry." I closed my eyes, shaking my head. "I can't control it sometimes and it-"

"Here," he said shortly. My bag landed beside me. "Take your stuff and leave, before the others get back."

I stared up at him. "But, I-"

"Just go!" he yelled.

The sound of a slamming door interrupted us, and we both turned towards the noise.

"John?" A voice called out, echoing through the warehouse.

John froze, then whispered at me, "Just go, I got this."

All the stories I'd read about the Witches and the horrifying tales of what they did to their own kind that broke the rules or turned against their own, I couldn't leave him here. I couldn't let them blame him for my escape.

I stood and grabbed my bag, slinging it over my shoulder quickly. John would probably hate me for this, but at least I'd know he would still be alive to.

Footsteps on concreted grew louder

"There's another door behind that section-" he started to say, but I cut him off as I grabbed him in a chokehold.

"What the hell?!" he yelled, grabbing at my arm.

"I won't hurt you. Just play along," I whispered as the newcomer walked around the edge of the rows of plants.

He was a tall man, dressed in a suit that I know Nathan would have drooled over. But his shocked and panicked expression turned to harden anger as he pushed forward with a shout.

"John!"

I raised my free hand palm up. "Stop right where you are." As I spoke, I concentrated on the heat of my power and focused it into the palm of my hand. The newest trick Poe had taught me. Forcing the Talent into a neon green flame that looked every bit the sickly poison I envisioned it to be in my mind. "Don't come any closer."

The newcomer froze in his tracks. His eyes widened as he looked at us, his hand shaking slightly as he held it out. "Whatever you're thinking, we can work this out. Just let him go."

Oh, I didn't like this. He was too scared. Maybe the fire was a bit much?

"I'll let him go once I'm out of here safely." I started moving backwards towards the door John had pointed out. The man mirrored us, on edge.

"John, has he hurt you?"

"I'm okay."

"John-"

"Seriously, Dad, I'm fine. Just do what he says."

'Dad'? Oh great. This was going perfectly down the drain. I turned and pushed John towards the door.

"Unlock it." I took a step back, keeping my eyes on both of them. I knew John and his father had their issues. We'd had too many late conversations about that in the dorms, minus the whole family legacy thing. But I didn't want to push John into escaping with me. I'd probably done a well enough job of 'staging' the whole hostage thing to get him off the hook.

John got the door unlocked and pushed it open. "There, now go."

I stepped over and grabbed his arm, pulling him along with me as I backed out the door.

"Wait! Let him go!" John's dad called through the door as

we left. I let the fire die in my hand. The last thing I wanted to do was actually burn one of us with it.

"I thought you were going to let me go," John said, angry, as we quickly crossed the asphalt heading for the gate.

"I will. I just need to get a bit farther." I pushed him in front of me, making him duck under the chains holding the gate closed.

Poe screeched overhead as we ran across the road, and relief flooded me at the sound. I knew he wouldn't have abandoned me. He flew lower, following my path away from the building.

"A way out of here would be really helpful about now," I yelled, keeping my eyes on the uneven footing as we ran across the sand dunes.

"Who the hell are you talking to?" John tried to pull his arm free of my grip. "Look, you're free, now let me go."

I glanced back. John's father had left the building, standing on the other side of the gate still, with his cellphone out, but he was far enough away that he couldn't hear us.

"Look, John, I'm sorry about this. I didn't- I didn't know you'd be here. I don't want you to get hurt, and I didn't want the Witches to think you'd helped me escape."

"But I did, or I was going to until you took matters into your own hands." Something twisted in my chest at the hurt in his words, and I shook my head. "After the stories I've heard of how Witches treat traitors. I didn't want that to happen to you."

That made him pause, his expression calculating. "What stories?"

I just shook my head, there was no way I could get into that now. Poe screamed again, and I felt the portal connect to the earth behind me.

Besides Avery, John was my only other true friend in the world, and I knew this very moment was the end of that friendship. There was no way a Necromancer and a Witch could be friends.

"Thanks," I said, "for everything." I turned to go, but he grabbed my arm, pulling me back.

"Just answer something for me."

I looked back at his dad and saw that he wasn't alone anymore. More figures in red-trimmed robes had joined him. It looked like they were chanting.

"If you make it very, very quick."

"Did you really have to kill someone to gain your power? Like for Necromancers in general, not just you."

His question caught me off guard. Why was he stuck on this killing thing? Did they all think we were a bunch of mindless killers? "John, Necromancy isn't something you can buy with death. It's something we're born with, and I've never heard of a Necromancer taking a life - at least, not outside of the war."

He still had that calculating look in his eyes, but our time was up. I watched his dad and the other figures take aim, raising their arms and pointing in our direction.

"Really gotta go now," I said and looked to the sky for Poe. He circled above us. "Let's go!" I shouted at him. A moment later, the sand next to me exploded like a landmine. I shielded my face with an arm, my ears ringing from the blast.

John pushed me towards the portal. I could see him shouting something at me, but couldn't hear him. That's when something struck me in the chest, throwing me back into the portal and into darkness.

Chapter 7

I was ejected out the other side of the portal, rolling in the dirt until something hard stopped my momentum.

I hurt. My arms screamed at me, the scars from my challenge weeks ago felt fresh on my skin and added to the painful wounds from the Witch's chains. Keeping my eyes closed, I tried to breathe. At first, I couldn't hear anything, but then sounds started coming through. I heard birds, frogs, and insects that weren't those of home or even from the grove of trees close to Avery's house. They sounded like I was somewhere much further away.

I shifted, putting my back against the trunk of the tree that had acted as my hard stop. I opened my eyes and groaned. We'd ended up in the Half-world.

The air was cooler than last time, but I still peeled off my hoodie to keep the humidity of the jungle from suffocating me. My vision blurred. All I wanted more than anything to focus on the back of my eyelids. But the thought of another beast coming across me like this was enough to push me to my feet.

Rubbing at my face, I had to force myself to concentrate. What needs to be first? The portal; had to make sure the portal was closed. I quickly glanced around, trying to see or sense it, but there was no sign. A weight lifted, and I took a deep breath. Bright side: I didn't need to worry about the Witches right now. But there were two figures on the ground between me and where I thought the portal must have been. Two? That wasn't right.

I stepped closer and knelt down to the small, black shape. There were feathers scattered everywhere.

Reaching for Poe, I hesitated, afraid I might hurt him. I sat in the dirt, looking for any sign of life in the bird. His breathing was slow and labored.

"Urgh." The other mound stirred in the corner of my vision. "What, where the hell are we?" John asked, pushing himself up.

I took a deep breath and tried to stay calm. At least I knew for sure he'd be safe from his family.

"It's another plane of existence, another world," I said absently, reaching again for Poe. We needed to find shelter and help if we could. That meant I would have to move him anyway. I glanced back at John. "You don't look so surprised at what I said."

John shrugged and stood, moving closer to me. "I knew there were places like this, I just never thought I'd actually get to see one. Oh, man. Looks like the poor bird took the brunt of the spell."

"He's not just 'a bird,'" I snapped, gathering Poe into the corner of my left arm, using my hoodie as a cushion.

I took another deep breath and tried to focus on one thing at a time. "That spell, what was it?"

"A basic blast spell, I think. Fire magic really isn't my thing."

I smoothed down some of Poe's feathers that were sticking up at odd angles. A sound caught my attention from our right. Something moved through the underbrush, coming towards us.

I stood quickly, putting myself between John and whatever was walking through the bushes.

"What's that?"

"Something is coming." I held out my hand, pulling at the last dredges of my power. I watched the big fronds twitch and move, and finally part to reveal an old man. The same one who'd found me after my Test. He was panting, leaning heavily on his knotted walking staff.

I breathed a sigh of relief, dropping my hand and power to cradle Poe more securely as I started to shake.

"Hassim," the old man said, bowing to me. "I feel portal open. Came as fast I could." His eyes fell to Poe in my arms and he hobbled over. His hand hovered over Poe's still form. "Hassim, this bad. What happen?"

John stepped closer. "It took the full blast of a spell. I've no clue how it blocked the whole thing, as small as it is."

The old man took a good look at both of us and nodded. "Come, Hassim. You need rest."

He started back into the underbrush, not pausing to see if we were following.

"Can we trust him?" John asked.

I glanced around for my bag. I'd been wearing it when we were blown through the portal, but I didn't have it now. "I do. He's helped me before, I think."

"Are you looking for this?" John picked up the messenger pack. The strap had ripped.

I reached for it, awkwardly shifting Poe in my arms.

John shouldered the bag and shook his head. "I got it. Just lead the way before we lose him altogether."

We followed the old man through the jungle as the afternoon sun beat down through the trees. We only walked for twenty minutes or so before coming upon a gathering of huts that I recognized. The big difference was the village was bustling, full of people moving between buildings, cooking food, talking. Children ran and screamed and played, dodging the grownups and livestock with practiced ease. I noticed that all the damage the Kastem had caused had been mended.

It felt weird to be back. Why would Poe bring us here and not back to the Mansor's ranch?

As we walked through the village, people grew silent, staring as we passed. Then the whispering started, and the bowing. The word 'Hassim' was repeated over and over.

"Uh, what's happening?" John whispered. He looked a little unnerved by the attention we were attracting.

The old man looked back at John. "He is Hassim. In your language, it mean 'Savior.' He won the beast that came to destroy and saved us all."

"Not all," I said gravely, thinking of the girl who'd fought so bravely before I could gather my wits.

John quickened his pace, trying to keep even with me to see my face. "It's true that you saved them, though? That you fought to protect them?"

I ignored his questions. I didn't want to deal with the misconceptions or what the Witches had brainwashed him into believing about Necromancers. I was worried enough about Poe. He'd never, as long as I'd known him, had been injured or sick. I'd always thought that had been weird growing up, but now that I knew he wasn't just an ordinary bird, it made sense. The only thing now though was, could he die? Would he recover from the blast that John's dad had thrown at us?

The old man, who introduced himself as Tamner, led John and me into the last hut on the edge of the village. It was bigger than the others but still modest. Rough glass jars and vials filled shelves against the earthen walls. Woven rugs and furs lined every inch of the dirt floor not taken by the large fire pit in the center.

"Set him there," Tamner said, pointing to a mound of furs built up into a bed. "Hassim, I need you close. Please do not go far."

I followed his directions, setting Poe on a bundle of furs as the Tamner hurried to search the shelves. He selected a few vials and one of the jars, and a bunch of things I couldn't recognize. Following the old man's direct would be simple. I wouldn't leave until I knew Poe would be alright.

"You, friend of Hassim," Tamner called over to John. "Come. Hold."

John stood inside the doorway, looking awkward and out of place, before walking over to accept the handful of items the old man held out for him.

"Tell me. What happened to your teacher, Hassim?"

He knelt on the other side of Poe, examining him closely.

"We were attacked. He opened the portal to take us away from the danger, but then..." I trailed off, trying to make my brain focus.

"The bird blocked most of a power blast, but the force knocked us all back through the portal." John stood over us, still holding the collection of vials and the jar.

"The blast. Tell me every detail." The old man stood and pulled another vial off a far shelf and took it to the fire pit. He put a large pot of liquid on the fire.

"Um, okay." John closed his eyes. I could see his lips moving as he tried to remember.

"Basic spell. Fire Elemental. Levels initiate and above. Um," John paused, his closed eyes squinting in determined concentration. "It's a chanted prayer, to the spirits. The more people you have chanting, the more energy goes into the spell."

Tamner nodded in satisfaction and started taking the items from John.

"Three others were standing with your dad, John," I added. "Would that make a difference?"

"Other than adding strength to the spell? No, not that I know of."

John watched the old man mix the quickly bubbling goo in the pot, but I caught the glances he tossed back at me. I could see the conflict in him. We used to be friends, but what were we now? I couldn't see us as enemies. Even if we were on different sides of the war, he had helped me escape, and I would do the same for him if the situation were reversed.

"The bird is pretty important to you, huh?" John said slowly, glancing away.

"Poe has been with me my whole life. He's family."

John examined the vials in his hands as he spoke slowly, "What I've been told about your kind, about Necromancers, isn't adding up to what I've seen in the last few hours. I just - don't know what to think."

"John," I paused, trying desperately to figure out a way to not sound like an insensitive monster. "I know we have to talk about it, just not right this second?"

He looked back at me a moment longer and nodded before sitting on the floor next to the fire.

"Hold him up," Tamner said, kneeling next to me with a small bowl and a thin, hollow reed. He sucked up some of the liquid from the bowl into the reed, using his finger over the end to keep it from draining. Then he carefully placed a few drops in Poe's open mouth. He sat back and gathered his things before taking them to the shelves.

"Now what? Is that it?" I asked. Poe's breathing grew more labored as if he were fighting for each breath.

"We wait." He gave me a solemn look. "It is all that we can do."

I didn't like the way that sounded - the grave, finality in the old man's voice. Poe had been there for me my entire life. He had helped me find my power and was helping me learn to control it, teaching me to use it. And after all that, I suddenly realized, I barely knew him.

Poe's limp form blurred in front of me, and I closed my eyes.

I opened them at the sound of cloth rustling to see John taking a seat next to me. Quickly, I rubbed at my face like I was tired. I didn't want him to think I was weak.

He set my bag between us, pushing it a little closer. "Thought you might want it," he said with a shrug.

"Thanks."

"No problem."

Tamner bustled about the hut, returning a few items to their shelves before grabbing the pot and ducking quietly out the doorway.

"I'm sorry." My voice sounded rough.

"For what?" John asked.

"For everything. Going to the warehouse was my idea. If we hadn't gone, Poe wouldn't have been hurt, and you wouldn't be trapped here with me."

He stared at me a moment, taking in my words. "Trapped? What do you mean 'trapped here'?"

"Poe is the only one who can open the portals." Well, the Vault could open a portal too, but that wasn't going to help us now.

John looked between Poe and me with disbelief. "The bird opened the portal to another plane of existence? You mean you didn't bring us here, the bird did?"

I didn't get a chance to reply as Tamner returned and settled in front of me with another bowl. This one was filled with a foul-smelling paste.

He gestured for my arm. I held it out for him, amazed to see it crisscrossed with blistering burns. I lifted the other as well to find it looked the same. I mean, I'd noticed they hurt, but I guess by this point I was numb to almost everything.

John stared at my arms a moment before looking away.

I flinched as the paste stung my skin, and had to resist pulling my arms back. "What's in that?"

Tamner shrugged. "You do not need know."

"How can I thank you, after everything you've done."

He wiped his hands clean on the edge of his robes and waved off my appreciation. "Nothing is too great trouble for Hassim. Not for Tamner." He pointed at the paste on my arms. "Do not touch. Rest, sleep is best."

Tamner left again, ducking out the hut, but John stayed, settling into a more comfortable spot so he could lean against the back wall.

"Tamner is right. You should rest. I will keep an eye on him"

"That's okay," I said, shaking my head.

"Seriously, Ezra. You look like death. Get some sleep. All our troubles will still be here when you wake up." John gave me a lopsided grinned and started peeling off his no-longer-white robe. Was he really the same person with the same bad jokes? Could I still trust him?

I wasn't so sure.

Laying back, I closed my eyes. I don't remember trying to sleep, but the next thing I knew, John was shaking me, roughly. "Ezra, wake up. Something's wrong."

I shot up, instantly alert. Tamner knelt on the other side of Poe, trying to hold the bird down. Poe shrieked, the sound piercing.

"What's wrong?" I reached out, intending to help the old man hold Poe, but as soon as I touched Poe's black feathers, though, I could feel his power building.

"I don't know, Hassim," Tamner said, struggling.

"Let go," I said, stepping back.

John stepped forward to help as well, but I grabbed his arm. "No, stay back." Poe continued to thrash about.

Tamner looked up at me in confusion. "Hassim, he'll hurt himself."

I grabbed Tamner's arm as well and pulled both him and John away, back towards the fire.

"Just wait. I think he's-" I didn't even get all the words out of my mouth before feathers exploded across the room. Then there was a groan of pain.

Poe's human form was very still and very pale against the furs he laid on, his clothes torn and dirty from the blast. I rushed back to his side, checking first to see if he was breathing. Tamner wasn't two steps behind me.

"What-" John stuttered. "What did I- where'd the bird go?"

"This is the bird," Tamner spoke as he examined the sprawled body, not bothering to face John. Poe stirred but didn't regain consciousness.

I waited, anxious to see what the old man would say. When Tamner finally turned to me, he smiled.

"He will be well, Hassim, although it take time for him to heal. Maybe long time. His injuries great."

I did not like the sound of that. "We'll have to find another way back, is what you mean."

Tamner nodded.

"Is there another way back?" John asked, stepping closer.

The old man looked to me. "Only the Blessed Hassim and the Great Ones have the power to travel between the worlds."

John looked at me. "He calls you 'Hassim,' does that mean you can get us home?"

I sat down by the fire, the panic and exhaustion catching up with me. "Poe mentioned that possibly, one day, I could open portals like he does. But I'm nowhere near that point in my training. I wouldn't even know where to start."

I thought about what Tamner said, how the Hassim and the Great Ones were able to travel between worlds, but it didn't fit with the Stanwood legends. The Stanwoods didn't always have a familiar to guide them. In fact, Poe was the first true familiar they'd had.

"Wait, how many others came here before me? Was it just Poe?"

Tamner shook his head, and eased back to a more comfortable sitting position. "Used to be many. The Blessed Hassim who walked between the worlds with the Great Ones. But in my great grandfather's time. They spoke of war in their world, one that brought much sadness to their hearts. We watched their numbers dwindle until they came no longer."

He looked at me. "I was young child when I saw the last. It is how I recognized you. I felt your portal, like so many years ago, and sent my granddaughter to guide you to us."

Tamner's words hit me hard. I already regretted my hesitation on that day, more than I regretted anything else in my life, but to learn that she had been his granddaughter... It felt like I was living the night all over again.

He looked at me with sorrow in his eyes. "Hassim, a great many tragedies will fall in your life, but there are wonders too. We must find balance between the two, lest the heavier pull you under."

I glanced away from him, not able to meet his gaze.

"I will go find something to eat. Food will help." Tamner left John and me alone.

John shifted, trying to stretch his legs out where he'd settled near the fire. "I wondered what had happened, you know," he said after a minute or two of silence. "You didn't answer any of my emails or phone calls. It was like you had just vanished off the face of the earth."

Looking away, I shrugged. "I've been home. Remember how I told you we didn't have a computer or cellphones? Reception is non-existent up on our mountain. We have to go down to the nearest town about an hour away."

He stared at me. "You're telling me you haven't left your house in three months."

I shook my head. "Not until recently. I left on a road trip with my dad earlier this week, but other than that, no."

He looked at me like I was crazy. "Your family is that scared of us? That you barely leave your home?"

"When we've been hunted to the last four of us, yes!" I snapped at him. Although, as I said that, I had that odd feeling of knowing they aren't my blood, even though I referred to them as my family.

John was quiet for a while after that. Only the sound of the fire and Poe's labored breathing filled the hut.

"They were right about you, though," he said finally.

I glanced through the flames of the fire at him. "What?"

"About being a Necromancer, I mean. The Priestess thought it was a long shot, seeing a Stanwood name pop up on a student loan form. They choose me because I was the closest and the easiest to get into college."

He laughed a little. "We tend to focus solely on developing our powers. We don't study much else beyond that, just enough to get through high school and complete whatever orders are passed to us from the Priests and Priestesses. I was kinda the odd one out in that respect.

"They arranged for us to end up as roommates and even take a few of the same classes. I couldn't tell you how nervous I was that morning, moving into the dorm. I'd never even seen a Necromancer, let alone have to take one out all by myself."

I looked at him sharply. "You mean, you were supposed to kill me?"

He looked guilty. "But I didn't, obviously! As soon as I met you and knew you weren't a Necromancer, I realized someone had to have made a mistake somewhere. There was no way I would have gone through with it."

I stood on shaking legs, they felt weaker than before. "But

you would have, right?" I accused around the tightening lump in my throat. "If I actually had any Talent then, you would have killed me. Just like any other Necromancer you might have come across."

John bit his lip, forcing his eyes up to meet mine. The truth was there, plain to see.

I turned on my heel and headed out of Tamner's hut.

John was asleep when I returned to the hut, which was probably a good thing since I didn't know what to say to him. I took an empty spot on the floor where the rugs and furs seemed thicker and lay down. As tired as I was, I still had trouble going to sleep. I was exhausted, yet my mind kept running in circles. I kept trying to think of ways to get home, or a way to let Avery know I was still alive.

Instinctively, I reached out, testing our connection. Felt ghostly, like the impression furniture leaves on the carpet after you move it. I could sense where it should have been, but that was all.

Closing my eyes tightly, I took a deep breath and another, trying to keep my panicking emotions in check. What was I supposed to do now? There was so much going wrong, I needed to find something positive to focus on.

I was still alive. Poe was still alive. Even if he was injured, he would eventually recover. And John was safe from his family.

Those thoughts finally allowed me to drift off to sleep.

The sun shining in my face woke me the next morning. Tamner stood in the doorway, tying back the rug that had kept the light at bay. I winced, sitting up slowly.

"Bright morning, Hassim." The old man sat next to me, handing over a bowl of brightly-colored chopped fruit I didn't recognize. It looked like cubes of watermelon but had the texture of a banana. I eyed it wearily.

"Eat," he said, picking up his own bowl.

I wiped the sleep from my eyes, glancing over at Poe. Tamner must have sensed my worry. He set aside his own bowl. "He is still resting, Hassim. It may be a while before he wakes again."

"Where's John?" I asked, changing the subject. I noticed he wasn't in the hut.

Tamner shrugged. "He a strange one. He is not like you, Hasim. I do not think one such as he has ever come here ."

Of course not. I don't think necromancers and witches have ever been civil long enough to broach a conversation, let alone travel together. "No, I doubt any of his people have crossed over here before."

I chose to focus on my food, taking a tentative bite. The fruit was slightly sour, reminding me of cranberries. Even with the odd texture, I finished the bowl rather quickly, and Tamner handed me another. After I ate and cleaned up in the little river near Tamner's hut, I wandered the village.

Women and children worked and played outside their homes. Some were cooking or skinning meat from animals I didn't recognize. I passed one group of boys, older than the other children playing between the huts, but not quite yet in their teens. They sat together, weaving baskets of dried reeds.

I tried to talk to a few of the women, but they only giggled, speaking a few words I didn't understand and shied away. It seemed Tamner was the only one who spoke English.

I continued through the village and came across the men, older boys, and a few of the women of the village sparring. They fought with spears and knives. I hovered, watching them from the edge of the clearing.

One of the older men noticed me, and after laying his opponent in the dirt, he came over to join me.

"Hassim," he said with a bow, then pointed to himself. "Suon, son of Tamner."

"Hi," I said awkwardly. "I didn't mean to interrupt. I'll leave," I said and turned, but Suon stopped me.

"No. Join us. You Hassim. You fight, yes?"

I felt a little unsure of myself. I'd only been training with Poe for a few months, but I was itching to do something besides sit, walk, or think.

I accepted Suon's invitation and started spending my mornings with the men. I'd never fought with any kind of weapon besides my power before, so when one of them handed me a spear, I looked at it with a bit of apprehension. Trying to use one while sparing with the men had them rolling with laughter. They set the younger boys to teach me the spear and the proper way to hold a knife with a lot of pointing and miming.

But when it came time to fight hand-to-hand, I held my own with the men of the village. There wasn't any laughing after my first fight when I landed a guy slightly older than myself in the dirt at my feet. There were only nods of approval.

Days passed, and Poe's condition didn't change. Tamner said it was a natural reaction to the injuries he'd taken. I still worried, though. His power, what used to feel like a raging storm in my mind, was now only a trickling stream.

I didn't see much of John. He returned to Tamner's hut in the evenings. He would eat with us then promptly go to sleep for the night, not saying more than a few words of thanks to Tamner. I'd watch him from where I meditated in the corner. After the first night, I found it hard to sleep. Instead, I'd review the lessons Poe had given me before, or I'd try to decipher the meanings of the incantations from the Reinhardt book I'd stashed in my bag.

John and I didn't speak much, and often what we did say to

each other was tense. I hated it. The distance between us was suffocating, but I couldn't think of how to break this standoff that we'd come to.

On the fifth morning, after sparing and washing up in the river with the other men, I finally worked up the courage to visit the one place I'd been avoiding. It was a little way down the river, where the water pooled into a swimming hole before continuing into the jungle. I could hear a waterfall hidden among the trees.

They'd buried the girl beneath a flowering tree, with bright orange blooms but vicious looking thorns hidden amongst its leaves. Something told me that mirrored the girl's image well. A beautiful but tough being.

I sat on an outcrop of exposed rock nearby and thought on how that day months ago had changed me. How I had failed to save her, how she had been so fierce against such a frightening creature.

"Tamner told me what happened that day," John said, coming up behind me.

I took a deep breath to calm my heart and turned to look at him. He'd come from the village, but his eyes weren't focused on me. They were glued to the small cluster of rocks that were placed around the outline of the girl's grave.

"He told me how you fought a demon and saved the village. He told me that is how all of your family gained their powers; by saving his people.

"But that's what confuses me. You're a Stanwood. They bring the dead back to life and kill with zombies."

"We don't kill!" I said sharply. "Or they don't."

"Which is it?" John asked, coming to sit on a tree root near me. "How can you be a summoner and a Stanwood?"

I thought carefully. John could use everything he's learned, anything I told him, against me, against other Necromancers. But- something had to change, right? John had everything wrong. Could it be that the war our families were fighting had all been because of a misunderstanding? Were we so ignorant about each other's worlds that it just sparked more aggression?

"I was adopted by the Stanwood Family. They found me as a baby, they didn't even tell me about being adopted until - I volunteered to take the Test."

"The test?" John asked.

"When a child with Talent is ready to be recognized as a full Necromancer, they can take the Test. It's a big right of passage for us."

I could see the judgment in his eyes, him trying to decide if I was as dangerous as he'd been told. I wondered if he saw the same look in my eyes.

"My Dad, he didn't want me to take the Test, because I wasn't a real Stanwood. He was afraid that I would die, but I was determined to take it anyway. But instead of taking the Stanwood test, Poe brought me here. I guess back to where all the other summoners came." I pulled the necklace free from my shirt, studying the pendant in my hands. "I had no clue what I was doing. It was all instinct and Poe's guidance that got me out alive." I glanced back at the girl's grave. "I just wish I had figured it all out a little sooner."

We sat in silence, listening to the birds and the sound of the waterfall.

"The other Necromancers, are they like you?"

"Are you like the other Witches?" I asked back. "I don't personally know all the others. I know my family, and I know the Manser's; our families are close. But the others, I don't know them as well. Then, there are all the cousins and the odd occasion when a person develops power outside of the Families. I can't personally know them all."

He looked a little embarrassed. "Sorry, I didn't think about that."

"What about you," I asked. "Is it true that the Witches

make a human sacrifice to the full moon? Do you drink the blood of your enemies and save their organs for your spells?"

John looked shocked, disgusted even. "What?! No! Where did you even hear that?"

I shrugged. "My brother told me when I was younger. I was pretty sure he was making it up, though."

John chuckled weakly. "We don't do anything like that."

"What *do* you do?"

He stayed quiet, watching his foot trace designs into the earth.

"Oh, come on. You already know what I can do," I said.

He raised a finger at me, then pointed down at the design. He didn't speak or do anything I could have seen, but I felt the ground hum. I sensed rather than saw the drop of power he sent to the drawing, and not a moment later, a seedling appeared, growing up from the dirt into a healthy sapling of a tree.

"My affinity is with the element Earth. I can grow things like this without anything but my power, but I can also heal the damage done to the earth. That takes time, but the rewards, the way the earth sings after it has been renewed, makes it all worth it."

I stared at him, amazed. I'd never seen power used like that before.

"Our power comes to us like yours. We find it as children and grow into it. Although there is no separation between affinities and families, like Necromancers have. We are sent to the Head Priestess on the first day of the year after our 6th birthday, and she sees in us which affinity we have. My mother is an Adept of Wind, and my father a Priest of Fire." John smiled. "They were so sure I'd take after my Dad, but..." He shrugged. "I'm kinda glad I didn't, you know?"

I was about to ask him what he meant when Suon came running up the bank from the village.

"Hassim!" Suon called as soon as he saw us. I could see in the way the man held himself that there was something wrong like he was about to face an opponent during our morning sparring sessions. I stood to meet him.

"Hassim, a beast in a village. North from here. Long walk. They ask for help. Hassim, you join us?"

Fear gripped me, but I fought it down. I would do this, no question about it. I knew what I was getting into now and what I was facing, but what frightened me the most was not having Poe with me. I took a deep breath and glanced at John.

"You're going?" he asked me, standing.

"I have to. I'm not sure I can explain it, but I have to." I turned to follow Suon back to the village but was surprised when John fell into step beside me.

"What?" he asked when I looked at him. "I can't join the fun, too?"

I shrugged. "I'm not sure I would call this fun."

Chapter 8

John and I followed Suon back to the village. I paused as we passed by Tamner's hut, briefly torn by wanting to check on Poe before we left. Suon noticed and nodded at me.

"Go, but we leave soon. Find us, middle of huts."

Suon continued on, but John lingered. "I'll make sure they wait for you."

I nodded and ducked into Tamner's hut. Tamner himself was by the fire, mixing herbs and medicinal plants. He glanced up at me.

"You go with Suon, correct?" he asked, turning his eyes back to his work.

"Yeah," I said, stepping over to check on Poe. His color was looking better, and his breathing was a little steadier.

"No worry about teacher. I keep a close eye on him." Tamner said as he appeared at my side with small two cloth bags. He raised the blue one, "Food," then the red one, "Medicine."

I watched as he added them to my messenger bag. He handed it to me by the newly fixed strap.

"Thank you," I mumbled, his kindness continuing to surprise me.

Tamner shooed me out of his hut, and I raced to join Suon and the others.

Women and children I didn't recognize gathered around the assembled warriors. Some held small bags or an armful of belongings, but most had only what they wore on their backs. When the warriors caught sight of me, they sent up a war cry that startled the birds from the trees. Then we left.

John and I walked with the warriors through the jungle. We tried hard to imitate their soft steps and make as little noise as possible. We didn't succeed by a long shot. Smoke filtered through the trees well before we come across any of the damage. The few huts and buildings that still stood were tinged black by the smoke.

"We split up," Suon, whispered as he came up to stand near John and me. "Go in pairs. Try and find it."

I nodded, and Suon turned to talk to the others in his own tongue. John and I started off, walking straight down the middle of the village. I tried not to think too hard about the body shaped piles of ash on the ground as we passed them.

"What are we looking for exactly?" John asked. "What kind of beast?"

A roof collapsed to our left, startling both of us.

"One that likes fire, apparently."

There's got to be a better way to do this. Then, I realized there was. I pulled out my pendant. "Stand back," I warned John and took a few steps forward. I concentrated and then pulled on the burning sensation that was my Talent. "*Vershala tulian das lo berruas.*"

The summoning circles appeared on the ground before me. The violent red lines pulsed as I concentrated on the words that formed in my mind. "*Kalha vas notha rak! Kastem!*"

I closed my eyes before the usual bright flash of light and

opened them to see Kastem. His many tails twitching with irritation. He sniffed at me and turned, before laying down in the dirt.

John stepped up to stand next to me, trying not to laugh. "You know, I thought I'd be afraid, but this was actually pretty funny."

"I'm so glad I could amuse you," I said dryly before returning my attention back to Kastem.

"*Akvito Kastem, don bval*!"

He just flicked his tail at me again, then rolled in the dirt. I put my face in my hands. This was a nightmare.

"Do you have any control over it?" John asked.

"I thought I did. But thinking back, I'm worried it was all Poe's influence."

John was quiet a moment before speaking again. "Uh, well, you might want to figure something out quickly," John said and pointed.

I followed his gaze and saw the pair of glowing embers in the trees. Large, bright orange wings expanded and lifted the bird-like beast from its perch in the tree. The size reminded me of the pictures I'd seen of an albatross, but this one was on fire.

"Oh, no..."

"We're out of time for sarcasm," John replied in a panic. "What do we do now?"

"Run!" I grabbed his arm and pulled him around, running back towards where we'd last seen the others.

"Suon!" I called his name a few more times before I heard a distant reply back. The bird dived at us, and I pulled John between the last two huts standing together.

"Exactly what are we supposed to do?" John asked, gasping for breath.

I peeked out, searching. The beast had disappeared into the

smoke. "We need to trap it, or hold it still long enough for me to get close to it."

The beast flew by again, stirring the air as a stream of fire spewed from its beak.

"Oh sure, that's not going to be a problem at all," John said. He glanced away from us, but then retreated back further into the alleyway. "You distract it, I'll make it sit still for you."

"Be careful!" I called after him.

I peeked out of cover again, trying to see which way the demon had gone. Kastem was still out in the middle of the village, sunbathing in the one spot of light that filtered down through the canopy and smoke.

The forest had gone strangely quiet. I couldn't hear the other warriors from the village, I couldn't see or hear John either. I stepped out of my hiding spot, never settling my gaze on one place too long. The heat from the burning trees and houses only added to the miserable oppressiveness of the jungle humidity. I searched through the smoke, trying to see anything as it drifted in, blocking my view.

A massive weight landed on my back and pushed me down as a screeching mass of heat swept by overhead.

Kastem let out a growling roar over me, shifting his weight to lunge at the flying demon.

I rolled to my feet, trying to find the flying bastard in the smoke. Kastem appeared at my side again, but this time he was ready, defensive. His whole body was tuned to finding the threat to us.

With a silent command, I asked Kastem to guard before closing my eyes and focusing solely on my power. I could do this, I had been training for months. I had already done it once to begin with. Kastem was proof of that.

Pushing any lingering uncertainty aside, I gathered my power into the palm of my hand. Without opening my eyes, I scanned the area near me. I 'felt' Kastem at my side. I felt each of the warriors, each a faint flicker of light in my mind's eye as most searched for the demon. Two were laid out, alive, but wounded. John was the next entity to catch my attention. His power flared violently green in my mind, reminding me of the green flame I'd called to my hand when I'd taken him hostage. It saturated the earth at his feet and spread, like a tsunami crashing into the shore.

Kastem growled and drew my attention away from John. Opening my eyes, I ducked as a shadowed shape dove at me through the smoke. I threw the power I'd gathered at it like I remembered from my first trip to the Half-world.

The bird-like-demon dodged it, circling around to strike at me again. Its wings swept the smoke away, and I got a clear look at the creature. Bright red feathers covered its body with a mane of orange and yellow feathers streaming from its head and long sweeping tail. Add in that it loved spewing fire, and it was the pristine image of a phoenix.

It was nearly on me when I realized I'd been too caught up in looking at it that I hadn't readied anything to throw at it. I ducked again as it swept past me, but watched as it turned around.

The earth trembled as vines shot up out of the dirt. They wrapped themselves tightly around the demon's legs and pulled the bird to the ground. More vines claimed its wings, pinning them to its body, as the bird screamed and spewed more fire in its fury.

"Now, Ez!" John yelled.

I shot forward, pulling my pendant and chain over my head. I wound around to its side, avoiding the burning bushes and its thrashing limbs as the demon fought to free itself from the vines.

I pressed the pendant into the beast's side. It screamed violently, dissolving into a glittering red mist. A whirlwind kicked up around me, pulling what was left of the demon into the center of my pendant.

One word whispered through my mind as I collapsed into the dirt with the empty vines. A name.

Sakava.

Struggling to catch my breath, I fought my way to my feet as the jungle fell silent. I turned to see not only John watching me but most of the village warriors as well. I dismissed Kastem, not wanting to take any chances of losing control.

"So, that just happened," John said with his eyes wide. I couldn't tell if it was fear or awe.

Cheers erupted from the men and women behind him as they rushed forward to surround me. Soun clapped me hard on the back, shaking my whole frame and bringing to my attention an entire set of bruises that I hadn't realized I'd gained.

"Well done," he exclaimed, his excitement almost overbearing. I managed a smile in response.

John let the impromptu celebration engulf me, but I felt his eyes trailing us as the group began to pull me back into the covering of the woods. I managed to free myself from the singing and cheering group as they started back towards their village. Waiting, I brought up the rear, not wanting to be the center of attention anymore.

"You're really a hero to them," John said, coming to walk beside me.

I shrugged, "I'm not a hero. I'm just doing what summoners have always done, what Poe has trained me to do. Besides, I'd have never been able to do it without your help."

John was quiet for a time, studying his feet as we followed the others. "So this is what the other summoners did? You came here and took the beasts that threatened these people?"

"That's what I've been told, but I've never had a chance to speak with another summoner." I couldn't keep the bitterness out of my voice.

"I think," John started slowly, "there have been a lot of misconceptions between Witches and Necromancers. On both sides."

"You think?" I snapped back at him. He held his hands up.

"I'm just saying." John was quiet a moment as he stuffed his hands into his pockets. "My whole life, I was told stories about how evil Necromancers are. How we have to protect the regular, non-magic community, to be their line of defense. And that meant we had to take a ...proactive approach." He shook his head, wrinkling his nose. "That's what my dad always said. I never thought much about it. Not until I was sent to be your roommate. There were nights I couldn't sleep. I kept thinking, what if you were a Necromancer? Here was this poor kid from the country who barely knew anything about pop culture, but was super nice. You always put others before yourself."

"What? No I don't-" I tried to protest, but he insisted.

"You were always the first to offer help if someone needed it, even if you didn't know what you were doing. Always the first to volunteer in the dorm. It bothered me a lot, actually. It made me question exactly what it was we were supposed to be fighting, Necromancers, or our own fear?"

My pace slowed, letting John's question sink in. He was right, I knew it. There were a lot of misconceptions coming to light, making me rethink a lot of my family's beliefs. But was it enough to put aside multiple generations' worth of hate and killing? "I don't know."

John and I walked in silence for a few minutes before he spoke again. "After I found out about the plants, I wanted to leave, but I hadn't gathered my courage yet when you showed up."

I paused, staring at John as he continued past me a few steps. "The plants?" I repeated.

John looked back at me. "They're poisonous to people like us, people with powers. If you eat it or it gets in your blood system, it'll mess with your mind. You can still feel your power, but you can't reach or use it."

I stared at him. "That's terrible!"

"It's driven some of those they've tested it on mad."

"Why-" I stopped myself. I didn't need to ask why. It was right here between us. The Witches were afraid of Necromancers. If they could get rid of our powers, there wouldn't be a reason to fear us anymore. "That's wrong," I said.

"Now, you see why I wanted to leave. Ez, they're going to do something awful. They're going to offer a truce and poison all the Necromancers with a feast laced with the stuff. I've wanted to say something, but I-"

I took a few steps to close the distance between us and held my hand out to him. "Thank you."

"For what?"

"For questioning, for helping me escape. For not killing me back in college. For trusting me. You pick."

John laughed weakly, reaching out and gripping my palm tight. "Come on, we'd better catch up."

There was a big party in the works when we returned. The smell of meat roasting and the sounds of music and laughter filtered through the trees. I paused, looking at the growing feast.

"What's wrong?" John asked.

"They're going to make a big fuss over us, aren't they?"

"Us, no. You, probably. That's usually what people do for heroes." He grinned at me but followed my gaze back to the village. "I don't think there's going to be any way around it. You might as well as get it over with, then sneak off early."

I frowned.

John threw an arm around my shoulder. "Come on, let's get it over with."

He led the way down into the village, and the reaction when we got there was just as loud as I feared. The villagers swarmed us with cheers, and praises of 'Hassim' were shouted into the growing darkness. Hands reached through the crowd, all for the briefest touch of my shirt or hair. John was caught up in the chaos, too, but they didn't seem to see him. Did the warriors not see how much he helped? It didn't seem fair.

John must have caught my expression because he smiled and shrugged at me. "It's not a big deal," he shouted over the singing and cheers.

He might not have thought it was, but I was still going to explain it to Tamner. It didn't feel right taking all of the credit.

I was pushed onto a cushion, placed in a large ring of people sitting around a bonfire. The fire was massive, and even with the ample space between it and the circle of dancing people just in front of us, I could feel the heat.

Tamner sat beside me, and another man I'd yet to meet sat on my left.

"Head of the village, Naekas" Tamner said, as John sat on his other side. Once we were all settled, Naekas stood, raising a large, delicately carved staff high above his head. The music and dancing came to an abrupt halt. All that could be heard was the crackling of the fire.

Naekas addressed his people, speaking in the guttural tones of their language. Tamner translated just loud enough for me and John to hear him.

"We are twice blessed. We have seen the return of Hassim. He has done his part today as his ancestors once did before him. He saved another village from a beast. May he save many more." Cheers went up around the fire as he turned to me and bowed. "Our thanks is yours, Hassim."

I awkwardly returned the bow from where I was sitting.

"Let us eat."

A plate of food appeared before me and then the party really began.

I escaped the festivities as soon as I could without drawing attention, which took a while since the head of the village kept introducing me to his daughters. Finally, after mentioning something to Tamner, the parade of eligible women stopped.

I slipped past the front line of huts and walked around to Tamner's, my mind still full of what John had told me about the plants. I shivered despite the heat. To be able to feel my power, my talent, but not be able to use it. For most Necromancers, that would just be torture, but for me? To have it build and build -it would literally kill me.

The fire was barely burning in Tamner's hut. Poe still lay on his pallet of furs. His skin didn't look as pale or sickly as when I last saw him in the early hours of the morning. His breathing was even and stronger, as well.

Poking the fire back to life, I added another log before pulling my bag closer to search through it. I was looking for the Reinhardt book I'd brought with me. I knew it might be a long shot, but I had to see if it contained anything about those plants the Witches were growing. There had to be a way to get back home. And I could only home we could do it in time.

I read and tended the fire as the singing and dancing outside continued late into the night.

When I shifted sometime later, trying to find a more comfortable position on the rug by the fire, I noticed Poe studying me from across the room.

"You're awake!" I jumped up, moving closer to him. "Do you need anything?"

He frowned at me, raising a hand to his head. "Something for the pain?"

I smiled. "Sure, let me go find Tamner-"

He grabbed my hand. "It can wait. Tell me what happened. How'd we end up here?"

"Here? You mean you didn't bring us here?"

He started to shake his head, but stopped, wincing. "No."

I sat back down next to him. "But that doesn't make any sense."

Poe closed his eyes and tried to sit up.

"Don't, really. Let me go get Tamner. We can figure out what went wrong later."

He gave a small nod, and I jumped to my feet, rushing out of the hut. I had to navigate the mass of bodies as people danced and moved around the massive bonfire. I ran into John before I found Tamner. He held a rough, carved cup out to me.

"Ez, have you tried this stuff?"

I waved him off. "Have you seen Tamner? Poe's awake."

He sobered instantly, turning to scan the crowd as well. "There." John pointed to where Suon and Tamner sat with the Naekas.

"Thanks-" I started to step away, but he stopped me.

"I'll get him. Go on back."

Grabbing some food, I stepped back into Tamner's hut. Poe's eyes were closed, but he moved a little. I sat next to him, setting the food carefully to the side.

"Tamner will be here in just a moment," I said.

He nodded but didn't open his eyes.

"How long have I..." he trailed off.

"Five, almost six days," I said.

He looked at me, blinking. "We need to get back," he started to sit up again, but stopped, staring past me. His eyes widened in surprise and fear.

I followed his gaze to see John standing in the doorway.

"Uh, Tamner is on his way, just thought you'd like to know." John ducked out, leaving Poe and me in silence save for the crackling fire. I could see the tension in Poe's body as he fought to stay upright.

"A witch. In the Half-world..." His voice had the harsh sound of anger, but it lacked energy.

"John isn't the same as the other witches. He actually *helped* me escape the warehouse." Even before I finished speaking, I saw the disbelief on Poe's face.

"He is a witch, Ezra," Poe labored to speak. "As much as I want to end this damned war, you can't trust them. Bloodthirsty monsters who've killed hundreds, if not thousands, of Necromancers. To bring one *here*? To the sacred Half-world?"

I leaned back, licking my lips. "John has had plenty of time to kill me. While we've been here, at the warehouse, even when we were roommates in college." Poe looked at me sharply, but I kept going. "He hasn't done anything, but help me the entire time. He may be a Witch, but he has been nothing but a friend to me."

Standing, I walked out before I said something I might regret. Tamner passed me, giving a worried look before heading in to see his patient.

I sat, bracing my back against the side of Tamner's hut. I couldn't fault Poe's reaction. He'd been protecting me since I was born, and John *was* a Witch. There was no way around that.

We had to get home, and John had to come with us. The information he had on the plants and other Witches was too valuable. But if my family's reaction was anything like Poe's, they would probably kill him on sight, instead of listening.

John sat next to me and passed one of the roughly carved cups into my hand. "You look like you could use this."

I looked at the cup in my hand for a split second and downed the contents without a second thought. I just had to remember that I shouldn't try and cast anything tonight. No drinking and summoning.

"Wow, I didn't think you needed it that bad!" John laughed as I finished the drink. It tasted like stale beer on the verge of going to the dark side, but my lips were immediately numbed as the warmth spread through me.

"Thanks." It wasn't a solution to my problems, but it made me feel a little better at the moment about having to deal with them later. I didn't need to think about how my family would react to John until we had a way home.

"How is he?" John asked.

I shrugged. "Tamner's with him now."

"Do you think he's well enough to create a portal home yet?"

I shook my head. "I don't know. Doubt it."

Tamner came out, leaning heavily on his staff. He took in the sight of us, sitting next to the door of his hut. "He is as well as he can be. He sleeps now."

"Thank you."

Tamner disappeared back into the hut. I looked out into the night, at the still dancing villagers, and tried not to feel. Poe would be alright. Now, all we had to do was find a way home.

"Come on," John said, pulling me to my feet. "Let's get some more of this awful beer."

―――

I woke up the next morning with a blinding headache. Sitting, I found myself in the middle of the village. Others were scattered around as if they'd fallen asleep in the middle of the party.

John was sprawled not ten feet away, his snores echoing in the quiet morning. I forced myself to my feet and walked down to the river to sit on the river bank and splashed fresh water on my face. It didn't ease the pain in my head completely, but it did help. The sun was glaringly bright off the water, so I closed my eyes against it. Sleep threatened to roll me under again, but I fought it. Instead, I sought comfort in meditation. My Talent was restored from yesterday's fight, and it itched to be used.

I calmed my thoughts, focusing on the exercises Poe taught me. Those days in the Vault felt like they were years ago—

My eyes shot open.

The Vault had brought me here the first time, not Poe. Could there be another place like it?

I rushed back to Tamner's hut, barely pausing to enter like a normal person. Tamner sat by the little fire, eating his morning meal. He turned to me and nodded as he finished his last bite. I sat next to him.

"In my world, there's a special place, a Vault. It has the power to bring someone here. It's how Poe and I first traveled here," I explained quickly. "Is there a place like that? A place with the power to send us home?"

He looked at me in confusion and turned to look at Poe, who answered his unspoken question in his own language. Poe was sitting up, leaning against one of the hut's supporting posts.

"Ah," Tamner said after Poe finished translating. "One, but it difficult to reach. Long journey."

"How long?" I asked, my hopes growing.

"A month or two, on foot," Poe answered. "It's high up in the mountain range that surrounds the jungle here. And not only is the road long but dangerous. Not all the people in this world are as nice as those here."

My heart sank; that wasn't any help. "Damn."

"We will find another way." Poe's voice sounded as tired as I suddenly felt.

I shook my head, "We don't have time. We need to get back and warn the Families before it's too late."

Poe sat up straighter with a grunt. "What do you mean? Too late for what?"

"John told me about the plants we found. The Witches are going to offer a truce and throw a feast to celebrate. Except the food is going to be laced with a poison that blocks out powers."

Poe's eyes widened. "How's that even possible? There's nothing-" Poe stopped himself. "How?"

"John told me about it, and I saw the plants with my own eyes," I said, defensively, staring him down.

He looked away first, but it didn't make me feel any better. Instead, I felt dread starting to build in me. Was there really nothing we could do to warn the others? "Is there another way back? Anything?"

"They may not believe the Witch's truce," Poe started slowly. "Your father and the other Heads may decide not to trust them."

"But what's to stop them from finding another way to poison them?"

"Nothing," John said from the doorway. "They won't stop until all the Necromancers are dead."

Poe watched him with a steely gaze. "I'm sure you would know."

John shrugged and moved further into the hut, taking a seat near Tamner, who watched us all with nervous glances.

"I can't speak for the actions of my family or our relatives and the other witches," John said. "All I can do is just what I am. Offering what information I have, and being here rather than with them," he paused, taking that moment to accept a bowl of food from our host. "Now, what are we going to do about getting back to our world?"

Poe shook his head. "There is nothing we can do. Not until my power returns."

John frowned at us. "So Poe has the knowledge, but not the capability to complete the spell. What about you, Ez? Do you have enough power to cast it?"

"I don't know," I shrugged, confused. "Does it even matter? I can't even learn-"

"Does he have the power?" John asked Poe.

Poe nodded slowly. "He does."

"Then we just use an Instruction Spell. Once Poe is feeling up to it, you merge your powers, your minds. Poe could then use Ezra's power as he would his own."

"No. That's no-" Poe started to protest.

"I'm just saying it's a way to get home that's faster than waiting until the sun burns out."

I watched them, confused at their exchange. "Wait, what's wrong with doing it that way?" I asked.

Poe and John continued to stare each other down, before Poe finally said, "It's not exactly the best or easiest way to go about it."

John scoffed. "It's doable and the fastest in our given situation-"

"Not with the potential side-effects!" Poe argued.

I raised an eyebrow at John. "Side-effects? What side-effects?"

John glanced away from me. "Nothing crazy-"

"Like reading another's thoughts or seeing their memories. Some people like to keep those things private!" Poe's anger bristled to the point that if he had the power to spare, sparks would be flying. He closed his eyes and took a deep breath before continuing. "Besides, I'm not exactly human anymore. Who's to say it would even work with me?"

"Look," John said, raising his hands in defense. "We want to get home in a hurry, right? I just offered an option. All we'd have to do is try or not."

I watched Poe settle back down in the bed of furs.

"Out of the question," he snapped. "We'll find another way."

Chapter 9

I avoided Tamner's hut most of the day. Poe made it clear that he wouldn't talk about trying John's way of getting home any further. Which made absolutely no sense to me at all. Wasn't getting back and warning the others of what the Witches were planning more important than some side effect that 'might' happen? What was he afraid of me seeing?

The villagers were cleaning up the party, some moving slower than others. I pitched in and helped, picking up discarded rough-cut cups and lost items. Then I moved on to help pack supplies for the refugees that would be returning to their village over the next day. Anything to keep busy.

Soun and I met with the other warriors in the training clearing late that afternoon, stretching and doing easy drills. John even joined us, surprising me when he easily tossed Suon into the dirt multiple times.

By the time we'd eaten the evening meal with the rest of the village and made it back to Tamner's, the stars were bright above us. I followed John as he ducked through the door covering, and settled in by the fire. Tamner was organizing the jars on one of the shelves, and Poe was asleep.

"He asked about you, earlier," Tamner said.

I rolled my shoulders, trying to ease the growing tension. "Is he doing better?"

Tamner nodded. "A bit."

"A bit isn't going to help us get home." John poked at the fire with a long stick.

"Fighting about how we're going to get home isn't going to help, either," I said, holding back a sigh.

Tamner replaced the last few jars back on their shelf and joined us near the fire. "He worries about you, Hassim. You like first of your kind. He wishes you safe."

"But what's the point of me being safe if none of those I care about are?" I picked up my book, picking at the worn leather cover. "It's not that I don't understand why he wants to protect me. I know I'm still very new at this, and I know I'm one of the last Reinhardts, but if my power was the difference between my family's and Avery's life and death? I have to protect them, just as Poe protects me. Because without them, who am I?"

John studied me over the fire, but I chose to ignore the look. Instead, I opened the Reinhardt book again and tried to understand what was written inside.

I opened my eyes the next morning to find Poe already awake. He sat with his back against the wall of the hut, blankets draped across his shoulders, and gathered around him. He looked at me briefly as I stirred.

"You're right," he said softly, looking back across the room at where John and Tamner had slept on the other side of the fire. Their beds were empty now, and I hadn't even heard them leave. "You both are."

Sitting up carefully, I found I was a little sore from sparing with the other warriors the day before. I didn't think about it long, though. I was too focused on what Poe was saying.

"We can't wait for you to learn the spell on your own or for me to recover. There's too much at stake." Poe leaned forward, struggling to adjust the furs on his shoulders before sitting back again.

"Why change your mind?" I asked slowly, not really understanding his one-eighty. "You were so against it-"

"I heard you last night," he said. "What you said about wanting to protect your family." He paused long enough to make me question if I should say something. But when he spoke again, he wouldn't look at me.

"There's a lot you don't know about me and the things I've done; things I'm not proud of." When Poe looked at me again, his expression worn. "Connecting together for the spell John suggests, it will open our minds to each other. You will be able to see memories from my past. It's not really a matter of 'if' it might happen, Ezra, but which ones you'll see." He paused a moment, looking away. "I'm afraid it'll change how you think of me."

I thought about it carefully, considering his reaction and how secretive he'd been since I found out about his second form. He'd been my very first friend, became my teacher when there was no one else to teach me, and now there was a chance to finally understand who and what Poe was?

I felt like he'd been hiding something, but could whatever it was really change my opinion of him? I doubted it.

"So," I said, "you'll do the spell then?"

He nodded. "We have to get back before those idiot witches do whatever they're planning. And as much as I do not like the method, it is the only way back quickly."

"How soon do you think you will feel up to trying?" I tried to keep the eagerness out of my voice. The last thing I wanted to do was rush him, but time was not on our side.

Poe eased himself back down to lay flat on the furs and blankets. When he closed his eyes, I noticed how much older he seemed. "Since it's your power we're going to use, how I feel won't matter. Get your things, and talk with the witch. By then, we can try."

After hunting down John and Tamner, and explaining, I gathered my things. I tried to wait patiently as everyone else got ready. Suon came looking for me when I didn't show up to practice with the other warriors.

"You're leaving," he said, without any preamble.

"How'd you know?"

"You look like a man eager to return home to his wife." He grinned at me. "I gather the others, they will want to see you off."

Suon walked off as Poe came out of Tamner's hut, a little unsteady on his feet. Tamner guided him out to the cleared space at the center of the village. John showed up shortly after.

"I'm starting to have doubts about going with you," John said. "Somehow, walking into a house full of Necromancers seems like a horrible idea."

I placed my hand on John's shoulder. "You have the information we need. I will make my family understand. Trust me, " I urged him, even though the look he gave me suggested otherwise. "I promise I won't let them kill you."

He sighed and moved the strap of the bag further up on his shoulder. Tamner had given it to him to hold his Witch's robe and a few supplies. "Just make sure you go through first."

Double-checking my own bag, I had the few things we'd come with. Suon stepped forward from the group of villagers that had gathered to see us off. He held a staff in his hand and passed it to me.

"Take this to practice with. Maybe when you return, you will defeat me."

I took it from him, holding it lightly in my hand, resting the end against the ground. "Thank you. I will practice, but I don't think I'll ever be able to beat you."

Poe placed a hand on my shoulder and gripped it hard. "We need to do this now before my strength fades more."

I nodded, turned to Tamner. "I didn't get a chance to say it last time I was here, but thank you for everything you've done to help us."

He waved a hand at me. "It is nothing, Hassim."

Looking over the small village, I was caught by the realization that I would miss this place, it's people, and the friends that I'd made here. And if the circumstances had been different, I might not have been so quick to leave.

I took a deep breath to steady my emotions and turned to John. "Let's give this a go."

"Close your eyes and clear your minds," John said softly.

I fell into the meditation quickly, breathing in the humid afternoon air and fighting to keep my emotions in check. I was too anxious about getting back, too nervous about how the others would react to John.

"Ezra, focus on your connection with Poe. Reach for him with your power and mind."

Doing as John said, I focused on Poe's presence beside me. I remembered the first time I felt the weight of his power. The time I saw him standing in the Vault. I remembered playing games with him as a kid. Extending a metaphysical hand, I reached for Poe, inviting him into my mind. A drop of his power similarly reached for me. When our Talent met, the sensation was different from anything else I've ever felt before.

Images flashed through my mind, like thinking about old memories except they weren't mine. I saw people I didn't recognize in places that looked vaguely familiar. I remembered the feeling of holding my children close, even though I didn't have any. I remembered fighting to my last breath to protect them and the rest of the Reinhardts as they were all hunted down like criminals.

I started to take a step back as I realized precisely what Poe was. No, *who* he was.

Don't break the connection, Poe's voice whispered in my mind. *I don't have the strength to help you reestablish it.*

But, I thought, *are you him? Are you really Allan Reinhardt? The last Head of the Reinhardts?*

"Focus," he said aloud in a strained voice. *We'll have time for 20 questions later. Now, show me your center where your power pools.*

It took barely a thought, and we were there. Standing at the edge of the cliff in my mind that overlooked my sea of power.

I don't know how this will feel, Poe said, but that was the only warning I got.

He reached right in and pulled as if he were trying to dig my heart out with a spoon. I watched as Poe manipulated my power, shaping it to form the portal home.

That's what we're aiming for. Build the portal in your mind, then fill the doorway with memories, thoughts, and things you know about the place you want to go. It's always easier to go somewhere you've been before, but going somewhere new takes a lot of effort and more power.

Instead of focusing on the Vault like I had expected him to, he concentrated on the flat, grassy pasture near Avery's home. I helped him add details, like the shape of the Manser's Grove and the different kinds of herbs her mom kept planted by the patio of their house.

My link to Avery flared to life with a burning sensation that nearly brought me to tears. I felt her sorrow, then surprise followed by such intense joy, my heart hurt again for an entirely different reason.

A murmur of voices sprang up around us like a whirlwind,

and I opened my eyes to find the portal standing before us, Avery's house in the distance.

I turned my gaze to Poe to find him watching me with a tentative stare.

You aren't upset, about finding out who I really am?

Surprised, yes, but upset? I shook my head, thinking quickly. *You're my great-grandfather. You knew my real parents, and you've protected me my entire life. Why would I be upset with that?*

His face relaxed, and he wavered a little on his feet. I felt him pull more of my power and feed it into himself. Poe's form twisted, morphing to the raven version of himself.

"Ready?" I asked Poe. He replied with a weak caw. I reached down and gently transferred him to my forearm, bracing him against my chest. "Let's go home."

Turning around, I caught sight of John. He was looking a little green in the cheeks.

"You know, now that I think about, I wasn't all too fond of that first trip. I could just stay here-," John started to say, but I grabbed him by the arm and pulled him into the portal after me.

The strange vertigo sensation was almost comforting. I was going home, even if that world was on the verge of an all-out war with the Witches, even if I knew my Family wouldn't be thrilled with John's presence, or what he had to say. I was going home.

I was going back to Avery.

Stumbling out of the portal, I caught myself with the staff Suon had gifted me with a gasp. I felt suddenly exhausted and drained, despite how ready I'd felt on the other side. I let the staff take most of my weight as John fell to the grass next to me with a soft thud and a groan. We'd come through in one of the Manser's pastures, just as Poe and I had pictured it in my mind. The sun was bright overhead, and the early summer heat was already building.

In the distance, I saw people running towards us, and one of them was Avery. Her excitement and anxiety filtering through the connection made her hard to miss.

We need to close it. Poe's voice sounded strained in my mind. I returned my attention to the portal as John picked himself up. The task of closing the link between the two worlds was much easier than it was to create. The summoning circles closed in on themselves, folding over and over in their intricate patterns until there was nothing left.

"Ezra!"

I turned as Avery slammed into me. She gripped at my clothes, holding me as tight as she possibly could. I'd just only managed to move Poe out of the way in time.

"I thought they'd killed you," she sobbed into my shoulder.

Pain that had nothing to do with the physical kind shot through my chest. "I'm okay," I tried to comfort her. "I wouldn't let them do anything like that. Where's Liam, did he make it back safe, too?"

She stepped a little bit. "Yeah, he's here. Caught a blast to his shoulder, but he'll heal."

"Who's that with you, Ezra?" Dad's voice was stern, and only slightly winded as he and Lyssa caught up with Avery. His eyes had fogged over white with the Stanwood power, his hands held out ready to cast.

"This is John, he helped me escape from the warehouse." I watched Dad's expression change from one of cautious relief to one of fear.

"You're a Witch?" Dad asked, making the simple question sound like an accusation.

John was very still next to Avery and me, his features still pale from the trip through the portal.

"Yes, sir."

I pulled free from Avery's grip and stepped in front of John. "He won't hurt us! In fact, he's had plenty of opportunities to kill me, and instead, he's saved my life more than once. He is not our enemy."

Lyssa looked at me like I'd grown another head. "He's a Witch! Of course, he's going to hurt us. It's just another one of their tricks to find us. To kill us all!"

John looked more frightened than a rabbit watching a greyhound as he stared at my father. "I promise, I swear it on the Earth, I mean you no harm." His voice shook a little.

"I don't believe you," Dad said. "Too many of your kind have broken their promises."

"Please, just hear me out. Then you can do whatever you want with me," John said solemnly.

I didn't think Dad could frown any harder. Poe struggled in my arms a moment, working himself free from my grip. He gave a soft caw and hopped over to John's shoulder.

"See," I said, pointing. "Poe trusts him. Isn't that enough to at least listen to him?"

The moment stretched out as Dad studied John, watching Poe's reaction to him. Finally, he lowered his hands completely, releasing his hold on his power.

"Fine. Bring him inside, and we'll talk, but no magic. If I sense even so much as a sliver of power from you, I will not hesitate to protect my Family. Do you understand?" Dad's glare at John made me shiver.

"Yes, sir."

"William, you can't be serious!" Lyssa argued.

Dad nodded. "We'll hear what he has to say first."

"But-"

"We can take care of him later, if needed." Dad stepped aside, motioning for us to go ahead of him.

We walked back to the house. All the party decorations had been put away, transforming the backyard into just that again.

Mom rushed out of the house as we stepped on to the back patio area, barely giving me a chance to brace myself before crushing me in a hug.

"I thought..." she started, but the rest was sobbed into my shoulder.

"Don't just stand there, come inside!" Avery's mother called from the door.

We filed into the house and claimed seats in the living room. John nervously taking the seat on my left as Avery sat on my right on one of the couches in the room.

Everyone stared at me with this expectant look, and I finally realized they were waiting for me to tell them what had happened.

I glanced at John before turning back to my parents, Evelyn, and Lyssa.

"It was all my idea," I started. "To go and investigate the information that Avery had received. It was really just extreme luck that Avery and Liam were able to escape at all."

Fresh tears shimmered in Avery's eyes. "I didn't want to leave you behind, but Poe made us return without you. I'm so sorry." She gave the bird a glare from the corner of her eye, which Poe ignored.

I shook my head. "You don't have to apologize. It was the right thing to do. I -" I paused, thinking carefully about how I wanted to phrase my words. "The Witches were stronger than I could have imagined. And what we found in the warehouse, I can't even fathom the possibilities if they'd gotten ahold of all three of us.

Avery gripped my hand tightly. "You mean the items that we found, the ones that looked like they were stockpiling for war?"

"No, it's worse. The plants we saw and what they can do." I turned to John, passing the reins of the story to him.

"The plants are something they been working on for years.

If ingested or exposed to your blood, it creates a metaphysical barrier between a magic user and their power, preventing them from using it."

"Why would they..." Lyssa started to say, but then it dawned on her. "No."

John looked down at his hands, clasped tightly in his lap. "Their plan is to call a truce and host a banquet in honor of peace."

Dad frowned. "Something tells me that banquet won't be as peaceful as it's supposed to be."

"They're planning a massacre," Evelyn whispered.

Silence fell heavily over the room.

"How do you know all this?" Lyssa asked John skeptically. "How do we know this isn't just some set up for another trap?"

John shrugged, and a helpless expression came over his face. "I'm an Earth Witch. I was in charge of the plants during the day, and I saw the others test them. I...I wouldn't wish that pain on anyone."

My stomach chose that moment to remind me that I hadn't eaten since the night before, and loudly. Avery stood and pulled me to my feet.

"Come on, let's get you some food -"

"We really need to discuss this more," Dad started, but Avery cut him short.

"I may be new at this, but this seems like it is something for all the Heads to discuss. And instead of talking ourselves in circles, and having to repeat everything when Nathan gets here, I'd much rather take the time to think on the best course of action."

Dad had a stunned expression on his face, but he nodded. "Very well."

Avery glanced past me, at John. "Are you hungry, too?"

"Yeah," he said, looking briefly at Dad and Lyssa before standing slowly, and following us to the kitchen.

"Sit, I'll fix you something," Avery said.

"We could fix it ourselves," I said, moving to grab a plate.

Avery glared at me and pointed at the table. "Sit. You look like you're about to fall over."

I took a seat at the kitchen table as Avery opened the fridge. John sat next to me.

"What happened that night after you got away from the warehouse?" I asked her.

She paused her search in the fridge and glanced back at me. "I wanted to go back and find you, but Poe had already created a portal, and Liam pulled me through before I got to say two words."

I sighed and released the tension that I didn't know I'd been holding on to. "I'm just glad you made it out of there."

She came over and wrapped her arms around me. "I'm the one who should be saying that." Avery kissed the top of my head.

"Perhaps I should leave the two of you alone to catch up," John said and started to rise from his seat.

Avery straighten. "Oh no, don't!" She went back to the fridge and continued fixing plates of leftovers from the party we'd skipped out on. Her hands slowed a moment before she spoke with her back to us.

"What I don't get is why a witch would help one of us." She slid the first plate into the microwave and hit a button, before turning to look at John. "I mean, don't get me wrong, I'm very grateful for what you did. I just don't understand."

John glanced at me, then looked at Avery. "Because I already knew Ezra, and I knew that he isn't what everyone, what all the Witches," he clarified, "said Necromancers were. I knew he wasn't a killer or a monster."

Avery pulled the plate from the microwave and slid it in front of him with a fork. "Wait, you already knew Ezra? How?"

"John and I were roommates at the college I went to before

I took the Test. I thought he was normal, and he thought I was, too."

"That's insane!" She pushed another plate of food into the microwave and started it. "That's got to be more than a coincidence."

John started to say more, but I spoke over him. "I think it was the will of the Gods."

For some reason, it seemed like a bad idea to let them know that John had been initially sent to college to kill me.

Avery brought our plates over and set them in front of us. "Well, whatever it was, thank you, John. I owe you my life." She smiled at him with tears shimmering in her eyes.

He nodded, blushing a little over his plate.

We ate in silence for a few minutes while Avery fixed herself a cup of tea and joined us at the table.

"Were you at the warehouse the whole time you were gone?"

"No," I said around a bite of food. "We left the day after they caught me. Something went wrong with the portal, and we ended up in the Half-world, instead of here."

"I knew it. That's why I couldn't feel you. That was the hardest part. Everyone kept asking if I could feel you, and if I couldn't-" Avery closed her eyes and took a deep, shuddering breath. "I didn't want to think that. But the longer you were gone, the more I believed they had killed you."

I reached for her hand and squeezed it tightly.

The sounds of raised voices carried over from the other room. One voice, in particular, stood out. I closed my eyes and scrubbed at my face with my hands. "Urgh, I really don't want to deal with him right now." Nathan was the last person I wanted to face, and while he may have wanted to mend fences before the ceremonies, that only left me unsure of the terms between us. Was he going to be civil to me now, or was the whole deal with the ring a one-time apology?

When I looked up, I found John standing, a look of concentration on his face. "I know that voice," he said.

We followed him back down the hall to the living room but watched as he peeked around the door frame instead of going in.

"You know who's voice?" I asked him, afraid I already knew the answer.

Nathan's voice rose above my father's again, questioning his decision in letting a Witch live, let alone listening to what that Witch might have to say. Just not in so many nice words.

John looked at me. "That one. Who is he?"

"That's Nathan," Avery answered, "Head of the Ackland Family. How would you know him?"

The color drained from John's face. He snuck another look around the corner of the door frame, then headed back to the kitchen, not waiting to see if we'd followed.

"You're kinda starting to freak me out," I said. "What's going on?"

He paced, moving around the table. "I don't know how, but that man in there isn't who he says he is. I don't get it. I can sense he's a Necromancer, just like you, but when I saw him a few weeks ago, he was a Witch. How is that possible?!"

I stared at him, trying to comprehend what he was telling me. "Nathan was at the warehouse? Are you sure it was him? Not someone that looked like him?"

John stopped and looked at me. "I'm very sure. He - he was the one who insisted on testing the plants on people. He brought in a Necromancer he caught himself for just that purpose."

I looked at Avery, but she shook her head. "All the Mansers have been accounted for. Between the betrothal and the Ceremony, we've been able to reach them all."

John looked at me, but I shrugged. "The Stanwoods are all here."

"But the missing summoners? And the other families?" John asked.

"No, not that I know of. The Heads would have mentioned if one of their Family were to go missing. There's too few of us now. "

"If that was Nathan that you saw at the warehouse, you don't think he'd turn over one of his own line?" Avery asked.

"I'm still having trouble believing that he'd betray us at all," I confessed, taking my seat back at the table.

"Really?" Avery exclaimed. "After all the hell that man has put you through your entire life? After he nearly forced me to marry his son? Are you mad?"

I took a breath, trying to think of a way to tell her about the little chat I'd had with Nathan the first day I'd arrived here at the ranch.

"He had his reasons." Her glare told me I should try harder to explain. "Nathan and I had a talk after I got here before the Ceremonies. He explained a few things, and I could understand, in part, why he treated me the way he did."

Avery looked as if she'd swallowed a dragon and was about to spew fire. I held up my hand to stop her from interrupting. I dug into my pocket.

"He also gave us a gift." I opened my hand, showing her the ring I'd chosen. Her eyes widened. "He had a whole case, full of rings. I tried to turn him down, it just didn't seem right to accept one. But when I saw this one-" She reached out, picking the ring up off my outstretched palm. "I couldn't say no."

"Ezra, I -"

John cleared his throat. "If I could just borrow..." He stepped between us to pluck the ring from Avery's fingers before she could slide it on.

He studied it, turning it every which way, even holding it

up to the fluorescent lights in the ceiling. "How did he manage that?"

"Manage what?" I asked, a sinking pit growing in my stomach.

"I told you my magic is based around Earth, right? Well, metal and gemstones are as much a part of Earth as plants are. But what I see here is - I just can't figure out how a Necromancer could possibly produce a Witch's spell as intricate as this."

I stared at him. Of course, there was a spell on the ring. Why hadn't I suspected it? Nathan was so mean spirited, his sappy story should have clued me in right away. "What sort of spell is it?"

John studied the ring a moment longer before looking up at me in confusion. "A location spell."

"Why would he need that? It's not like he couldn't just contact us." Avery asked.

I shook my head, confused by the whole mess. "None of this makes any sense. Why would Nathan need to pretend to be a Witch? Or want a location spell on Avery?"

"Or maybe he wanted to know where you were?" John countered.

Dad and Nathan's voices grew louder, echoing in the hallway as they came closer to the kitchen. I looked at John. His eyes had grown wide in panic. "Will he recognize you?"

"I'd really not take the chance, thanks."

Avery snatched the ring back from him and stuffed it into her pocket. "Quick, take him out to the barn. I'll stall them."

I led John out the kitchen door and out to the little dirt courtyard by the stables.

Chapter 10

Poe called out weakly from his perch on the stable's roof as we made our way out the door. We didn't make it far before I spotted Liam in the courtyard talking with Collen. They glared at John as we passed by and broke off their conversation. Liam followed us into the stable.

"Ezra!"

I turned, and John paused beside me.

"Dad told me you'd returned. I didn't believe him when he said you were friends with a Witch." Liam's hostility caught me off-guard, though I shouldn't have been surprised. He'd hated Witches ever since he learned what they'd done to the Families.

"John saved my life multiple times, and I've no doubt that he'd do it again. I don't care what side he's from."

Liam pointed violently at John. "But you brought him here! He could be a spy! I wouldn't put it past a Witch to double-crossss us." Liam spat on the ground.

"I don't even know where 'here' is," John mumbled as he shifted behind me.

"Liam-"

"Dad should have killed him on sight." Liam turned on his heel and stomped away.

I shook my head and put it aside for now. We had bigger fish to fry. "Are you sure you recognized Nathan's voice? To be honest, I wouldn't put it past him to be working with the Witches, but I want to be one hundred percent sure."

John looked at me with steady eyes. "I'm sure."

"Right," I glanced around the stables. A few of the horses were looking out of their stalls, watching us with curious eyes. What were we to do now? All I could think of was to talk to Dad, and Poe. We had Witches with a killer plant determined to wipe us out at one dysfunctional dinner. And apparently, that would be with the help of someone who is supposed to be an ally. The whole situation was making my head hurt. What the hell was I going to deal with first?

I paced, then turned to John. "Wait here. I'm going to get my father."

"Uh, I'd rather not be alone on a ranch full of Necromancers who want to kill me. Thanks."

I tried not to laugh at my own stupidity. Of course, it was a bad idea to leave John alone. I looked around and saw the tack room. I scavenged a scrap of paper and pen, and scribbled a note before whistling for Poe. He flew in and landed on my shoulder.

Folding the paper, I handed it to him. "Give this to Dad and meet us in the Grove. We need to figure out our next move."

John and I made it out to the Grove without running into anyone else. I sank down into the soft grass of the clearing, stretching out as sleep threatened to roll over me. John stopped at the tree line, his eyes widening as he reached a hand out in front of him. He looked up from his hand and took in the scene of the Grove.

"What is this place?" he asked, fixating on the altar.

I debated for a moment, trying to think of how much I should tell him. I thought of Avery. It was her family's relic. What would she say?

"Each family has an object or a place that's sacred. It's something that connects us with our power, our ancestors. All the Necromancers that came before us. This is the Manser's Grove."

John lowered his hand, still in awe. "I can feel the power here." He closed his eyes, taking a deep breath. "It's ancient, pure." He frowned and looked up at me. "I've felt this before, around our own sacred items."

"What items?" I sat up, willing my body to cooperate.

He shrugged. "The Priest and Priestess of Earth both have staves that give off power like what I feel here.

What John said about the power feeling the same as the Witches items. Did that mean they were the same?

I thought about it, staring out at the trees, and the longer I stared and thought, the more the idea felt 'right.'

Poe called through the trees and then appeared. He drifted down to the grass in front of the alter, shifting to his human form before touching the ground. He sagged, leaning against the stone, out of breath.

I jumped to my feet, ready to rush to his side, but he waved me off.

"I'm fine," he grumbled, pushing himself up straighter against the alter.

I still walked over and sat next to him, John still stood at the edge of the clearing. Poe gave a not so pleasant smile.

"Aren't you going to come closer?"

John glanced around, uncertain. "I could, but I don't think I should. I don't want to," he searched for the right word. "-trespass."

Poe closed his eyes. "It's probably for the better."

We waited in silence for the others to arrive. I paced in the clearing, trying to puzzle out what Nathan was up to. It didn't make any sense why he would be working with the Witches. He was most vocal about taking our chances to attack the Witches. So unless he was urging both sides to fight, which wouldn't-

My feet stilled as the realization came over me.

"What's wrong?" John asked.

"That's it," I said. "He's trying to re-start an all out war. But why?"

"What's this all about?" Dad asked, coming through the trees with Lyssa and Avery.

I swallowed, knowing how completely crazy this was going to sound, especially to Dad and Lyssa. "Nathan is working with the Witches. He's trying to force both sides back into an open war with each other."

Lyssa burst out laughing. "Nathan? I don't think so."

Dad only frowned.

"It's true," John said, "I recognize him. He's been to the warehouses several times, working with the High Council to develop the plants. Except, he didn't feel like a Necromancer then, I thought he was a Witch."

"You're both insane!" Lyssa said, wiping tears from her eyes. "Nathan is the most outspoken against the Witches. I can't see him looking at one without killing him, let alone working with one." John shifted, and she shrugged. "No offense."

"That's what I thought at first, too, but think about it." I stood and crossed the clearing, standing closer to them. "He's working with the Witches in disguise, and now they've got a weapon that could kill us all."

Dad's frown deepened. "Have you considered that he's working undercover for us? Gathering information on the Witches to warn us?"

"Then why hasn't he? From what John's said, they're almost ready to purpose 'peace,' but Nathan hasn't said a thing."

"It also doesn't explain the tracking spell," John said.

Poe stirred, pulling himself up to his feet. "Tracking spell?"

Everyone turned to John, but I answered. "Nathan gave me a ring to gift Avery with, for our bonding, but it's spelled, with a Witch's tracking spell."

Poe cursed, wavering. He barely managed to catch himself on the altar before he fell. I hurried over to his side, offering a hand for support.

"What's wrong?" Avery asked.

"He was hurt-"

"It's nothing," Poe interrupted. "This isn't the time to worry about my health. In either case, whether Nathan is on our side or not, the Witches are still planning on killing us. We need to prepare."

Avery crossed her arms against her chest. "I agree, and I want some answers."

"Can you see anything?" Lyssa asked, "Has there been any omens?"

Avery closed her eyes, a small frown line of concentration appearing between her eyebrows. The air around her shimmered with power.

"I can't make anything out. It's too uncertain, too many possibilities for my Talent to see them all," she paused, opening her eyes. "But Thea might be able to see something."

I turned back to Dad, who'd been rather quiet.

He nodded. "Let's talk to Thea first, quickly. Then Nathan. Either way, he has more information on the situation that we need."

Dad and Lyssa turned to leave, disappearing through the trees. Avery paused only a moment to squeeze my hand. "I'll find Thea. Meet you back here?"

I kissed her. "Sure."

Following her to the tree line of the grove, I stood next to John as she left.

"Who's Thea?" he asked.

"Avery's younger sister. She'll be Head of the Manser Family one day, once she's old enough. She has the strongest gift of Sight that any Necromancer has had in centuries." I smiled, remembering what she'd said only a few months ago. Finding my power and being bonded to Avery, it was all her doing. "I owe her quite a lot."

John looked back over my shoulder. "Is he going to be okay?"

I turned to follow his gaze. Poe had sat back on the ground again, resting against the altar with his eyes shut, his breathing labored. He even looked a little pale in the growing darkness.

But he'd been nearly wiped of his power when we'd arrived in the Half-world, then had used the little he'd recovered to meld with me to create the portal to return us here.

That gave me an idea.

"Keep watch for the others."

John nodded.

I walked back over to Poe and knelt next to him, slipping into the meditation with some difficulty. My body was tired, and asking it to do more spell work was more than it really wanted to do. I reached into myself anyway, going slightly deeper into my mind than I had the first time I'd tried this spell only hours ago. Gathering a ball of energy, I pushed it at him the same way we'd created the portal together. Except instead of filtering the power into a spell, I guided it to him and gave him a metaphysical knock on the door.

Poe stiffened, and with a deep gasping breath, took the energy within him. He closed his eyes and leaned forward, breathing heavier. When he opened them again, they were clearer and more alert.

He gave me a side-eye. "You shouldn't have done that."

I sat back and shrugged. Poe looked ten times better,

already sitting up straighter, looking more like himself. It was worth it.

"Someone's coming," John said.

A few moments later, Avery crossed the tree line, looking frantic. "We can't find her. She's gone."

I stood. "What do you mean, 'she's gone'?"

"Have you tried searching for her?' Poe asked, standing.

"Of course, I have!" Avery's glare at him could have melted ice.

"Through your connection to her as Head of the Manser Family?" he amended as he stood.

Avery looked liked she'd swallowed a sour candy. "No," she said.

She walked over to the altar to brace her hands on it. I walked around to the backside of the stones so that I could see Avery's face as she concentrated.

Seconds passed in tense silence before she let out a shout of rage, slapping the altar with her bare palms.

"Avery?" I asked, growing concerned

She looked up at me with tears in her eyes. "She's not here. Nathan took her."

I fought down the panic that threatened to squeezed my chest as we raced back to the house, only to find it frantic with activity. Dad was outside the back door, waiting for us.

"Liam is missing as well," he said, looking grim.

Avery stopped in her tracks. "What?"

"Nathan must have taken them as well." I scrubbed at my face with my hands. This was going downhill fast.

"Nathan?" Dad stopped as he caught sight of Avery's expression. "I see."

"I just don't understand what he wants with them!" I paced.

"Did you see where Thea was?" Dad asked.

Avery nodded. "A little. She was in a small room, like a

bedroom. There was a window, and I could see a forest and a lake out of it."

Dad frowned. "That sounds like the Ackland Estate. How did he get her out there that quickly?"

For a small moment, no one said anything. As the weight of what was unfolding before for us settled on our shoulders.

John asked quietly, "What now?"

I took a deep breath. "It's time for us to confront Nathan."

We talked through our plan of action and collected everything we needed to take with us. It was completely dark by the time we'd gathered again in the grove.

"Are you sure you can do this?" Dad asked again for the third time in the last hour.

"I'm reasonably sure. I did just cast it a few hours ago."

"With help," John added.

I shot him a glare and stepped into the center of the clearing. My grip tightened on the staff Suon had given me as I took a deep breath. I could, and I would.

I closed my eyes just as I felt Poe land on my shoulder. He started to meld with me, trying to sync his thoughts with my own. Mentally, I brushed him off. If this went south, we'd need his help later, and I didn't want to drain his power further.

A deep breath later, and I reached for my Talent, the power that pooled deep in my soul. It wasn't as much as when I was fully rested, but it had been a busy day.

I pulled at it, focusing my mind on the picture Dad had shown me of the Ackland's living room. I'd never had the pleasure of visiting their mansion in California, and the more I learned about Nathan, I was glad of that.

Holding up my hands, palms out, I started the incantation. The wind whipped around me as the summoning circle appeared, growing out from a pinpoint, slowly, as I fed my power into it and coaxed it into existence. It spun slowly, then wildly as I sped the incantation up. The circle turned slowly, growing, taking up the entire side of the clearing as it pulsed along with my heartbeat. Nathan's living room opened up to us, and I turned back to the others.

The look on Dad's face made me pause for a moment, trying to decipher it. It was something between awe and pride.

"Is it safe?" Lyssa asked, doubt clouding her expression.

I nodded. "It's ready,"

"Let's go, then." Dad stepped through, followed by Lyssa and Avery. I waved John through next. He went reluctantly, and Poe and I followed.

The house was eerily dark and quiet. The curtains were all closed against the late evening sunlight. I closed the portal as soon as I was clear of it. The kick-back of left over power caught me by surprise, dropping me to my knees and sending Poe up in a rustle of feathers.

"Ezra!" Avery was by my side immediately, but I waved her off.

"I'm okay, just need to catch my breath," I said as Poe settled himself on the mantle above a cold fireplace. He gave a soft caw.

"Or maybe you shouldn't have done that spell twice in one day," John said dryly.

I started to tell him where he could shove his comments on my casting, but Lyssa cut me off first.

"It's like no one here."

I took one last deep breath and climbed back to my feet with the help of my staff.

"Thea is here, I can feel it. She's close." Avery started to move for the open door that looked out on an entryway and grand staircase.

"Wait," Dad said, catching her by the arm. "We need to be smart about this. It's doubtful that they would leave her here alone, and who's ever here would have felt the portal. We should pair off and search. Poe and I, Ezra and Avery, Lyssa and John -"

"Oh, no," Lyssa interrupted. "You aren't sticking me with the Witch. I don't trust him."

I glanced at John. He shrugged, "I don't want to be alone with some random Necromancer, either."

"Fine," I said, "John and I will pair up. Avery can go with you, Lyssa."

She looked satisfied, but Avery looked impatient.

"Be smart and safe," Dad said. Poe cawed again from the mantle. Dad reached for him, helping him up onto his shoulder.

We split up. Avery followed Lyssa up the stairs to the second floor as Dad and Poe crossed the entryway and into what looked like a dining room.

I stepped out into the hall, glancing around. There was another doorway at the end behind the stairs.

"Come on," I said and led the way.

"I don't know why I had to come here with you," John said, his gaze shifting nervously along the walls and floor, almost as if he were afraid the house itself would attack him.

"I remember you saying something about not being left alone on a ranch full of Necromancers," I whispered harshly at him. I peeked into what I found to be the kitchen. How would Nathan react when we accused him of working with the Witches? My instinct said, very badly.

No one was in the kitchen, and a quick look out the windows showed that no one was out in the backyard. Dad came through the connecting door to the dining room, shaking his head.

"Nothing – "

A heavy thud came from the second floor, followed by a high pitched scream that caused us to jump. We rushed for the stairs, Dad was already halfway up the flight before I'd even made it to the first stair. I was two steps behind John, about to climb the flight of stairs myself when I felt it. The wave of uneasiness that washed over me, turning my stomach. It froze me in my tracks as the world swam. I must have made a noise because John turned around.

"Ezra?"

Closing my eyes, I gripped the railing tightly as another wave of passed over me, and another. I tried to concentrate, just for a moment, to figure out where they were coming from. It rolled over me again, stronger than any of the previous ones. The basement.

I slid down the few steps I'd made it up because I didn't trust my legs to hold me up.

"Ezra!" John followed me off the stairs and back towards the kitchen.

"Down," I barely managed to get out. "The basement."

Between John and leaning on my staff, we made it back down the hall to the kitchen, where we had to play guess which door led to the basement. We found the large walk-in pantry and the garage before finding the set of stairs that led down into darkness. The waves were coming faster, stronger. I could barely stand as John practically carried me down the stairs.

The basement was nearly bare. Flickering light from pillar candles clustered here and there on a concrete floor revealed exposed wooden framework and unfinished drywall. A table cluttered with tools and supplies was pushed into the far corner, next to an old fireplace mantle. A large mirror sat on top, covered with a drape so that only the bottom left corner was free to reflect light.

A large design was painted in white on the floor. The circles and sigils looked familiar, like the ones from my summoning spell. When we got to the bottom of the stairs, I knelt down and held a hand out over the painted lines. The power I'd felt pulsed from them, sending waves out and through me like a rolling surf. I looked out across the designs on the floored.

They weren't just like the ones in my circles. They *were* the designs. The exact same sigils, in fact.

"How in the world has he managed this?" I mumbled to myself. "How is it even possible? He's not a Reinhardt."

"You're right, I'm not." Nathan came around the only corner in the basement, back behind where the stairs led up to the kitchen. I could see a bunch of bookshelves and the vague shape of something else I couldn't quite make out in the darkness. "But I do have an impeccable memory, and blood Talent. And that, that is a potent tool."

I stood, wavering only a little as the world swam around me. John's hand steadied me.

Nathan circled around us, walking slowly towards the table, staying outside the painted lines. "Have the right kind of blood, and you can do anything. Go anywhere." He shrugged. "Be anyone."

"Where's my brother and Thea?" I demanded.

"Oh, I'm sure they're quite preoccupied at the moment." Nathan gave a nasty little smile. "I'm so glad you decided to join us, and who said a Necromancer and a Witch couldn't be friends, uh? Look at you two, all *Fox and the Hound*."

"I don't know, it seems to me like you've more experience in that area than I do." Focusing on standing up straighter, I tried not to give in to the pulse that wanted to pull me back to the ground. It screamed at me, urged me to feed my power into it.

Nathan raised an eyebrow up at me. "I see. That is unfortunate. I guess we'll just have to do this the messy way." He picked up a knife from the table and studied it for a moment, turning it this way and that to look at it in the candlelight. I recognized it as the Ackland's sacred item, the Blade of Shezmu.

"Do what?" John asked. I could feel him reaching into the

earth below us with his power. But I wasn't sure exactly how that was going to help us inside a basement.

Nathan looked at us. "Why, kill you, of course." Without warning, he threw the knife at John.

I dove to the side, but John didn't move. Instead, earth bubbled up, breaking the concrete on the floor to grow upwards, blocking Nathan's attack. I expected the knife to fall to the rubble, but it bounced, turned in mid-air, and shot straight for me. Before I could get over my surprise, the ground rushed up in front of me, blocking the knife again.

John popped up beside me, and we ducked behind the earthen wall.

"Let's give it more targets. If we can distract Nathan, it might stop whatever spell he's got on the knife."

I nodded, understanding. "I just need you to cover me while I cast."

John stood and ran across the room, drawing Nathan's attention, and the knife, towards him.

Taking a deep breath, I focused on the summoning chant, whispering it under all the noise John was making with the earth and concrete. But as I spoke the last few words of the spell, a blast knocked me back, breaking my concentration and sent my staff clear across the room. It sent me flying back into the wall. Pain exploded in my mind, sending stars across my vision.

When I could make sense of the world again, Nathan stood over me, the knife in his hand.

"I'm actually quite saddened by this, you know," Nathan said. "The last of your family, I'm not even sure how you managed to escape the Witches in the first place."

It might have been the concussion, but what he was saying wasn't making any sense to me.

"In any case, let me allow you to meet your real family."

Nathan closed the distance between us, the knife coming uncomfortably near to my neck.

I glanced wildly around for John, but it was Poe I caught sight of first, darting for Nathan's face with open talons.

Nathan yelled, bringing his arms up to protect his face. "Crazy bird!" He slashed at Poe. I took the chance to scramble to my feet and put some distance between Nathan and me.

Poe raked his talons along Nathan's knife arm, slashing open gaping wounds. He backed off then, flying around to my side before transforming to the human version of himself.

Nathan swore vividly and turned to glare at us, then froze. The color drained from his face.

"No," he said with a shaking voice. "No, this can't- You're supposed to be dead. I killed you!"

Poe grinned at him. "You're not wrong."

Nathan took a shambling step forward, his expression darkening. "How? How are you here? I watched them burn your body. I was there when they spread the ashes. You are *dead*." Nathan lunged at us then.

Poe pushed me out of the way and met Nathan head-on. They grappled, fighting hand to hand before Nathan broke away to throw a spell in Poe's direction, who laughed, knocking it away almost absently.

"I know your game, Lloyd." Poe laughed, "Oh, I'm sorry, you go by 'Nathan' now, right?"

"This is a trick," Nathan said, clutching his wounded arm. "You're an illusion, you can't be real!"

Poe's expression darkened as he stepped closer to Nathan, backing him into the wall. "I'm real enough to kick your ass," he said and hit him with a right hook that Nathan tried and failed to block.

"I'm real enough to see that you haven't changed." Another punch. "Real enough to get revenge for killing my family."

I stared at them. What?

"That doesn't make any sense," John said as if voicing my own thoughts. "The Reinharts were mostly all killed back before you, and I were even born, right? Nathan would've been what? A few years old, if barely that." he guessed.

"Don't let him fool you, Witch," Poe said. "This man is much older than he looks."

Nathan laughed. He looked slightly unhinged with his blood-stained clothes, swollen jaw, and hair disheveled. He looked just how I would expect someone to look like before they killed a whole bunch of people. He was not the clean-cut businessman I was used to seeing.

I glanced back at John and found him kneeling next to the sigils on the floor. They were untouched by the magic that he'd casted earlier. In fact, they looked as if they'd been burned into the concrete, rather than painted like when we first came down. How'd that happen?

"What the hell?" I sank to the floor, ignoring Nathan and Poe for the moment.

John shook his head. "There's something wrong with the magic here. It's..." he closed his eyes, frowning. "Tainted, twisted."

I knelt next to him, and reached to touch the nearest sigil.

"Ezra, no!"

I looked up in time to see Nathan take advantage of Poe's momentary distraction, slamming the blade in his side before stepping quickly back, pulling the knife with him.

Surprise fluttered across Poe's face, a hand going to the wound, only to come away red. He coughed, blood staining his lips.

"POE!" I dove for Poe's side as he fell to his knees, clutching the wound. Catching him before he could fall, I eased him to the floor. Blood soaked through his shirt and began to pool beside us.

Poe's eyes seemed to fog over as he focused on me. He

reached up and, with a finger soaked in his own blood, touched my forehead.

"*Quae quod unum genus sumus*," he whispered.

Darkness overtook my vision as my body burned with power, causing me to gasp. It burst out of me, racing out in every direction, searching.

I didn't understand what was happening, I couldn't control it, and I couldn't figure out what it was doing. I could only watch as the power spread over the city, and when it didn't find what it was looking for, it continued out over the country. It searched through each and every person we came across. Leaving no one untouched, until finally, the power struck a resonance, then another and another.

I saw them all, all at once. An athlete alone in the college gym working out. A pair of twins sitting up in their beds, staring at each other across their brightly decorated bedroom. A leather jacket-clad punk, out late in the streets of New York City.

The lost Reinhardt children weren't children anymore.

Just as quickly as the visions started, they were gone. However, the connection to the other Reinhardts was still there, similar to my bond with Avery, only fainter. Enough to find them. I could rebuild the Reinhardt Family.

I looked down, a million questions on my lips, only to find Poe was gone, his form shifted back to that of a very still bird.

Doubling over, pain, that had nothing to do with the physical kind, ripped at my heart. I set Poe down carefully, ignoring the dampness on my cheeks.

"I should have realized it sooner," Nathan said. "You never did look like a Stanwood." He gave a halfhearted laugh and wiped the blood from his mouth with the back of his hand.

I struggled to breathe. Poe was gone. My great-grandfather.

Rage flooded through me. Standing, I turned towards Natham as the smirk wilted from his face. He took a step back, and another, trying to keep the distance between us as I walked towards him. Throwing my hand out before me, Kastem appeared with a mere thought. I didn't have to say the incantation or struggle for control. He just materialized.

"You think a demon is going to stop me?" Nathan forced a laugh, but I could see the fear in his eyes. He knelt, slapping his blood-covered hand on the painted circle. His expression hardened. "Two can play at that game. "

The circle flashed a bright, eye-blinding white, forcing me to shield my eyes. The paint on the floor began to move, twisting and growing until the body took up most of the free room in the basement. The head of the snake-like demon rose to tower above us.

"Uh, Ez," John said in a hushed voice beside me. "We should find the others. We can't do this on our own."

Kastem growled. The snake's black eyes narrowed as its three forked tongue tasted the air. Nathan stood behind the creature, the fear in his eyes gone. He'd already figured a way out of this, the bastard! I couldn't let him get away with taking the others, with killing Poe.

"Keep it busy," I told John.

Giving Kastem one clear order of helping John take down the snake, I moved to the side, my attention on Nathan.

The snake dove forward, and Kastem slashed at it with his claws as John rolled away. I took the chance and jumped around it, heading for Nathan.

He grimaced, side-stepping back in an attempt to maintain the distance between us.

"Why?" I screamed at him. "Why would you kill your own kind?"

He sneered. "A child like you could never understand. The world has changed. We've been hunted since the first Necromancer discovered his power. First by the normals, then the

Witches. We've always had someone out to get us. The Witches were just better at killing us than the rest."

I pulled at more of my Talent, gathering it into my hand like I had back in the warehouse. "Then why the hell are you helping them?"

Nathan shifted the blade in his hand as if trying for a better grip. "Don't you understand? The whole system is broken. Necromancers, Witches, even the normals, there isn't any difference between us. It's just a matter of perspective."

I stared at him, the power forgotten in my hand. He was mad, but hadn't I thought something similar not too long ago?

"But to fix it," Nathan continued, "I've got to tear the system down and rebuild from scratch. Since the other Heads didn't agree with my vision, well, they had to be the first to go. Allan was particularly stubborn," he grinned at me. "I quite enjoyed killing him again. I suppose I have you to thank for that."

Blood pounded in my ears. Rushing forward, I clutched at my Talent, shaping it like Kastem's claws, I slashed at him. Nathan defended himself easily, the smirk growing wider on his face. It only angered me more.

I screamed, trying harder to reach him. Nathan laughed and backhanded me, sending me spinning to the floor. Kasten appeared, defending me from the snake as it tried to strike. Kastem pushed it back, managing to open a gash along its body. Black blood oozed from it.

John pulled me up to my feet, but I was already looking for Nathan. He was on the other side of the basement, drawing on the wall in blood.

I moved to attack him again, but the snake cut me off, forcing me to back up. Kastem flanked it, trying to drive it clear of my path.

"Well, it's been fun," Nathan said. "Be sure to give Allan

my regards." He saluted us with his knife and slapped his free hand on the drawing.

The wall melted away and revealed a dark forest path on the other side. Nathan stepped through, and the doorway closed, leaving us alone with the demon he'd called. At least that explained how he'd gotten here so quickly with the others.

"How are we supposed to kill this thing now?" John yelled at me. "We've only put a scratch on it!"

It dawned on me then that maybe we didn't have to kill it. Maybe there was another way we could deal with it.

"I need to get close to it," I said.

His eyes widened. "Do you really think that would work?"

"I've no clue, but it's my best idea."

At this point, I only wanted to reach the newly reformed wall Nathan had stepped through. Maybe I could figure out how to follow him or trace the power to figure out where he went. Anything.

Kastem pushed me out of the way as the snake's tail whipped around and almost clotheslined me.

"Focus, Ezra!" John yelled.

I ripped the chain from my neck, freeing my pendant to swing from my hand. The snake's black eyes were focused on Kastem as he swiped his claws at it's injured side.

The white serpent dove forward, striking at Kastem, and missing by a tail's width. I eased to the side, not wanting to face the creature head-on. The snake's head turned towards me, but John threw a piece of concrete at it.

"Hey, over here!" John pulled its attention away, letting me get closer.

I dove forward, slamming the pendent into the snake's scales. It shrieked, dissolving into a black mist that swarmed to the pendant's stone center. A breath of the creature's power whispered through my mind leaving the snake's name.

Louca.

Pain shot back from the pendant into my hand, burning as the metal grew white-hot. I dropped it to the floor, swearing.

The skin that was left on my hand where the pendant had been was white and leathery-looking. Not a good sign. Taking a deep breath, I surveyed the ruined basement. The wall Nathan had stepped through looked untouched, not a smear of blood on it. No trace of power.

Collapsing to the floor, I screamed in frustration. Nathan was gone.

John limped over, I turned away. This was all my fault. I should never have gone to that warehouse, should never have put others at risk. Poe was dead.

Punching the floor with my 'good' hand, I screamed again, the pain coming nowhere near to that I felt inside.

John sat next to me, his arm around my shoulders. He didn't say anything, but he was there.

Chapter 11

I swallowed past the pain my throat before glancing around the basement. Panic gripped my chest. "Where's Poe?"

Kastem padded over to a small amount of concrete rubble and pushed at it was with his nose.

"I didn't think you would want him to get hurt more," John said and made a flicking motion with his fingers.

A small flash of relief flared through me as the pile of rubble moved to show Poe, untouched by the fight with Louca. I struggled to stand, my body nearly refusing outright. John helped me up, and Kastem returned my staff to me, so I could lean on it.

Picking Poe up was difficult as I tried to use my injured hand. The burn had already blistered and broken, the wound weeping.

"What about your necklace?" John asked, standing over where it still lay smoking on the floor.

What was I supposed to do with it now?

After getting Poe settled in the crook of my arm, I walked back over to where John stood. Bending down carefully, I held my good hand out over the ruined chain, trying to see if it was still as hot as the pendant. It was warm but not unbearably so. I held it by the chain, careful not to touch the pendant.

"We need to find the others," John said, exhaustion in his voice. "They might need our help."

John led the way with Kastem and me in his wake. We ran into Dad on the stairs, his eyes going wide when he caught sight of us.

"What happened? I thought you were right behind us."

"We were," I said. "But then-" The words left me, I couldn't think of how I was supposed to say it. Dad hadn't known precisely who Poe was. I'd never had the chance to tell him about it.

John spoke for me. "Ezra heard something in the basement, so we went to check it out. We found Nathan. He tried to kill us."

"He got Poe." I clutched the bird tighter to my chest. "It was my fault."

Dad stepped forward and pulled me into a hug. "And Liam? Was he down there?"

I shook my head. "We didn't see him."

He swore. "We've searched the rest of the house. Liam isn't here. Nathan must have taken him somewhere else. I can't sense him anywhere."

"What about the missing girl?" John asked him. "And the others? Are they okay?"

"Yes, they're safe-"

"William," Lyssa called from the landing on the second floor. "You better come see this."

I dismissed Kastem, noticing the satisfied look in his eyes, before following Dad upstairs and down a long hallway to a set of double doors. On the other side was an office - desk, computer, a few bookshelves. Avery was looking over papers in a file folder with Thea.

"You're okay," I said with relief. I trusted Dad's word, but seeing it with my own eyes just made it real.

Avery looked up and dropped the file on the desk in front of her. She rushed over to me. "Gods, what happened to you?"

"Nathan got away," I said grimly.

"This isn't going to make you feel any better," Lyssa said and passed the folder to Dad. He started skimming through them. His eyes grew wide, his hands holding the files shook.

"What is it?" I asked.

Thea looked at me with tears in her eyes. "Liam's been working for Nathan."

I couldn't believe her. I stumbled back, dropping into a leather armchair. "Not possible."

John took the folder from my father's loose grip and opened it flat on the desk.

He frowned at me. "They're right, copies of emails between Nathan and Liam." John shuffled through the papers. "He detailed events-"

"Rituals that only a Stanwood would know, things that I taught him!" Dad shouted.

John continued. "And some handwritten letters, signed by Liam."

Was Liam working with Nathan? Did he even know what it was Nathan was up to? I stared at the mess of papers before me. What do we do now?

Avery's touch on my shoulder pulled me from my thoughts. "Ezra?"

Everyone was looking at me like I hadn't answered the first few times they tried to get my attention.

"Are there any other files like this?" I asked.

Lyssa held up a stack that would rival any college students require reading for a semester. "Got them all here."

Dad nodded. "We should get back then. I want to send out

an alert. Nathan, Liam, and any other Necromancer that might be working with them are not to be trusted."

Avery hovered close to me. "Are you able to get us home?"

The thought of another spell exhausted me, but this was something that only I could do, and I didn't much feel like spending the night here.

I staggered to my feet and nodded, "Yeah."

Taking a few steps back away from the others. "Everyone ready?" I started the spell using the doorway as a frame. Reaching for my talent wasn't the hard part, nor was I struggling to find the energy. Focusing, however, was nearly impossible. Trying to settle on an image, a place to come through on the other side, my mind couldn't decide.

Avery's hand rested on my outstretched arm, her presence helping me hone in on exactly where I needed to go.

The portal opened before us, and everyone but Avery filed through. Avery took my free hand and led me forward, but I don't remember making it to the other side.

―――

I slept for a day and a half after we returned. Mom didn't take the news about Liam well. Who would? I still have trouble believing it myself. Liam, a traitor?

Avery, John, and I drove to the Reinhardt house once I was feeling better, but they wouldn't let me take a turn behind the wheel. I didn't argue, not with the luck I was having with concentrating. I slept more instead, and tried to think more on our next steps. Where did we go from here?

We arrived late in the afternoon, the sun highlighting the white columns on the front of the plantation house.

"This is it?" Avery asked as we pulled up the long drive. "It's huge!"

Legacy of the Necromancer

"Nearly a hundred and fifty acres," I said.

Avery parked the car and cut the engine. It didn't seem like anyone had been here since Dad and I had left, but I couldn't be sure.

"Ezra?"

I looked down at the fresh pine box I held in my lap, pain as pure as the wood gripped my chest. "Follow me," I said and climbed out of the car.

I led the others around the house and followed the directions Dad had given me.

There was a thin path of worn away grass that wound from the back garden into the woods. We walked for about twenty minutes. The dim light of the afternoon sun filtered down through the trees and shaded the path. I'd begun to think that I'd gotten the wrong way when I caught a glimpse of the gravestones through the trees.

Stopping on the edge of the Reinhardt graveyard, I stared at all the markers, as if a forest of stone had replaced the trees.

Here, before me, were almost all of my blood relatives. Every Reinhardt that had been recovered was laid to rest here as my Family's tradition dictated. Their bodies cremated, a handful of ashes spread on the wind, and the rest buried.

Avery came up beside me, wrapping her arm around my side.

"Ready?" she asked.

"No," I said truthfully, but stepped forward anyway, searching for a particular stone. It was on the other side of the graveyard from where we stood, surrounded by his wife and children.

Standing in front of Allan's grave, a sea of uncertainty crashed through me. How could I ever take his place?

John moved beside me and knelt to place a hand on the ground in front of the gravestone. The dirt pulled away from him, sinking, creating a hole the perfect size. He stepped back, letting me move forward to set the pine box into the ground.

I stayed on my knees in front of the grave, trying to think of something proper to say, but words failed me. I could only stare at the box.

"I'm sorry," I said, finally.

Avery laid a single white lily on the top, and John knelt, his hand hovering over the ground, waiting.

I nodded, and John used his affinity with the earth to fill in the grave.

Avery and John left me there. I vaguely remember her mentioning something about unpacking the car.

Looking out over the gravestones, I found myself wanting, for the first time in a long time, the Stanwood Talent. Or even maybe Thea's gift. To look back at the past and see what they were all like.

Reaching out, I traced the letters on Allan's headstone, thinking about the other Reinhardt children as I cleaned out the dirt that had settled in the crevices. Had they had a chance to know their real families? Or had that been stolen from them, too?

In any case, it was time to call them home.

I sat back on my heels and sighed, lifting my pendant free from my shirt. Its new chain was bright against the ground as I set it down on top of Poe's grave.

I pulled my pocket knife from my coat and flipped open the blade. Closing my eyes, I looked inward past my connection with Avery to where my Talent now pooled in the center of a ghostly, web-like pattern. I took a drop of my power, and tossed it at the web, sending vibrations out to each of the four anchor points - one for each of the lost Reinhardts.

"Power calls to power," I mumbled and looked down at my hands. I cut the tip of my ring finger on my left hand. The blood welled up and I let it fall onto the Reinhardt necklace. "Blood to blood."

As the blood seeped into the pendant, the stone brightened, glowing a deep, rusty red. I felt the power rush through me, out along the web to each of the others. I could only hope that they would follow it home.

The Story Continues in
WILL OF THE WITCH

Visit J.D.'s Wattpad profile to read the current draft of Legacy of the Necromancer's sequel, *Will of the Witch*.

Sign up for J.D.'s Newsletter for updates on new releases and upcoming releases.

Also by J. D. Robinson

LIGHTWALKERS SERIES

Nocturnal

Darkest

Before the Dawn

Acknowledgments

I want to thank each and every one of you who've read this far. My readers and fans, my family and friends, all your support allows me to follow my dreams. THANK YOU! Big thanks also to my former Patreon fans for supporting my dreams!

Before I go, I want to take a minute to thank my very, most bestest friends for their love and support, (I know bestest isn't a real word.) Thank you, Jax McQueen. Your stories always leave me hanging on every word and laughing late into the night. I can't wait to see what you come up with next! Rachel Hamm, thank you for all your wonderful support. I *never* would have imagined myself to be a chicklit reader, but your stories are captivating, romantic, and just as fun to read a second and third time as much as the first! Paige Nguyen, thank you for all the wonderful afternoons chatting about writing over coffee and for letting me beta read your Woven Crown. Your fantasy speaks straight to my heart, and I'm eagerly waiting for your next big project. <3 Remy Alan, your friendship means the world to me and your work continues to blow me away. I can't wait to see what more you come up with. And last, but certainly not least, Sarra Cannon, who is such an inspiration and hero to me, I very much doubt I'd be where I am today without her and our original critique group.

About the Author

J. D. currently resides in North Carolina with her family. She's a world traveler, a foodie, a relapsing coffee addict, and a rabid fan of the dark & deadly. When not torturing her characters, she's playing taxi-mom and dissuading muggles of the notion that Hufflepuffs are the innocent, sweet, peaceful creatures they're portrayed to be. You can often find her at Starbucks.

You can find more of J.D. on her Wattpad profile: @Sachula, and more of her elsewhere at https://linktr.ee/sachula.

Made in the USA
Middletown, DE
12 August 2024